ALSO BY THE AUTHOR
Moth-Kin Magic

SMOKE FROM THE CHIMNEY

SMOKE FROM THE CHIMNEY

Kathy Kennedy Tapp

A Margaret K. McElderry Book
ATHENEUM   1986   NEW YORK

LIBRARY OF CONGRESS CATALOGING-IN-PUBLICATION DATA

Tapp, Kathy Kennedy.
  Smoke from the chimney.

  "A Margaret K. McElderry book."
  Summary: Erin relates the events of the summer
when she and her friend, Heather, discover the "real"
Tarzan and she becomes increasingly aware of the family
problems caused by her father's drinking.
  [1. Family problems—Fiction] I. Title.
PZ7.T1646Sm 1986   [Fic]   85-18713
ISBN 0-689-50389-X

Lines from "The Highwayman" from COLLECTED POEMS by
Alfred Noyes (Copyright © 1930, 1934, 1936, 1941, 1942, 1943,
1947 by Alfred Noyes. Copyright © 1920, 1922, 1925, 1927 by
J.B. Lippincott Company. Copyright © 1939 by Sheed &
Ward, Inc.) reprinted with the kind permission of Harper & Row
Publishers, Inc. and John Murray (Publishers) Ltd.

For Ken, with love.
For Alison, with thanks.
And for Mary, Sister Timothy and Johnny
—with memories.

SMOKE FROM THE CHIMNEY

One

■□■

Loud talking floated out the open window of Maddens Restaurant.

"Do you still think we should try it?" I whispered, looking up the trunk of the weeping willow.

Heather craned her neck to look up, too.

"See that limb at the top, Erin? It reaches right over the restaurant roof, just like I told you." She chewed her lip a minute, then looked at me. "If we can just get that far without anyone seeing us, we'll have the whole roof to ourselves. Our own boma!"

"*If* we can get up that far." I studied the willow again. It was a real hero of trees, growing right out of the downtown alley blacktop. With the walled-in river on one side, and the back of Maddens Restaurant on the other, it was completely hidden from the downtown traffic. I could see a few sawed-off places where branches had been pruned. But the main crotch was low enough to reach. And one limb did reach over the roof like Heather said. The tree looked climbable.

But there was that stretch of straight trunk, right outside the upstairs banquet room window. And all those people inside, eating—

"How come they're using the banquet room so early, anyway? It's not suppertime. School just got out."

Heather scowled. "Probably a tea or something. Bunch of ladies sitting around eating cake." Then she took a deep breath.

"Look, it's our test," she said in a low solemn voice. "If we want the roof for a boma, we have to earn it. Just like in E.R.B.'s books. Prove that we're true denizens."

I tightened the straps of my backpack and grabbed the lowest branch. When she put it that way, there could be no more hesitating. "We'll have to shinny up that straight part of the trunk," I whispered down.

"Not trunk. *Bole*. E.R.B. calls it the "bole" of the tree, remember?"

"Then we'll have to shinny up the *bole*."

I hoisted myself into the first crotch. The upper leafy branches swayed above me, thick, green, inviting. As I climbed, the scared feeling changed to excitement, to the thrill of facing danger, to the prickly-itchy feeling that broke over me whenever there was a wild or woodsy place to be explored. Jungle fever.

Of course we'd make it, window or no window, banquet or no banquet. We'd be as quiet and stealthy as Sheeta, the panther, melting against the tree.

The rough bark scratched my legs and arms with each scoot upward. I didn't feel like Sheeta at all, with my backpack humping out behind me and my heart banging around too fast, as I inched past the big staring window.

4

I stole a quick look inside. Heather was right. They were ladies. And they were eating cake.

I sent them silent brain waves; Don't look out the window. Concentrate on your cake. *Don't look.*

My shoulders ached. One of my shoelaces was untied. The strap of my backpack was cutting into my armpits. My nose itched.

"Keep going," Heather hissed from below. "You're almost there."

Two scoots later, my hands touched the upper limb. There was just enough strength left in my arms to hang on while I swung my leg over the crotch. Then it just took a few seconds to crawl out on the limb and drop down to the flat, black-tarred roof. I stood stock still, staring. I knew suddenly how Christopher Columbus must have felt when he discovered America.

"Hurry, Heather! You've got to see this," I whispered down. "I found—I found—" But there wasn't a good enough word to describe what I found.

The roof had two levels. I was standing on the lower part. The view of Main Street was blocked by the higher roof section at the front of Maddens. Adjoining buildings fenced in two sides. Thick, waving willow branches closed the fourth side in with green, closed it off from the rest of downtown. I couldn't see the back alley with its trash cans and store exits, or the brick walls that edged the river. There was just the dark water below and the drooping willow branches that made the whole world green and wild.

Heather dropped beside me with a thud and yanked off her backpack. Her green cat's eyes

5

gleamed. "Erin, it's perfect! It was meant for us!" Then she lowered her voice. "Our roof boma."

I pulled the cipher tablet out of my backpack and marked it down.

"Roof boma: shelter in upper jungle reaches. How's that?"

"Jungle shelter. Yeah," she said in a low dreamy voice.

I stretched out on my stomach and stared down through the branches, into the river. "*Our* jungle shelter."

"We can come here every day after school. We'll bring supplies in the backpacks."

"I need one like yours." I pointed to her green nylon pack. "It's a perfect camouflage color. Where did you—"

"Rummage sale." She grinned. "Where else?"

I grinned back. Heather's mom's rummage sale mania was a standing joke. All spring and summer she drove her Nissan wagon around town, following rummage sale signs like Sheeta on the scent-spoor of fresh meat. And she really sniffed out the bargains, even though the Prescotts had plenty of money. Some of the stuff she bought just to fix up and resell, like furniture. Other things she got because they were collectors' items. And that was how we got E.R.B. in the first place.

"These old Edgar Rice Burroughs books are getting to be real collectors' items," she said on that fateful day last March, when she lugged in the dusty box full of books with thick yellowed pages and half-rotted covers. "The old lady across town had a com-

6

plcte original set. The Tarzan series, the Venus series, the works. You can read them, if you like."

Heather had giggled and rolled her eyes and said, "Really now, Mom. Tarzan." And that would have been the end of it. Except that Heather does with books what little kids do in a candy store, or adults in a Chinese restaurant. She has to try every kind just once. Take a nibble of every single kind.

The nibble turned out to be a big bite. For both of us. Tarzan wasn't anything like the cartoons or the comic book versions. The real Tarzan, with his steel-gray eyes and great strength, was the true Lord of the Jungle. Edgar Rice Burroughs made it all so real. He pulled us right down into the steamy jungle, while Tarzan outwitted the evil men who plotted against him, and slew the wild beasts, going for their jugular veins and eating the fresh, blood-warm meat. And his son Korak was just like him.

Yes, we knew a lot about Tarzan. In three months we'd read half the Edgar Rice Burroughs box. Our E.R.B. box, we called it. We had our cipher tablet to mark each new jungle word as we learned it. Word like "Kudu"—sun, "Tantor"—elephant, and "Numa"—lion. And now we even had a true boma. Heather was right; it was meant to be.

I jumped up in a burst of jungle fever and happiness. "Come on. Let's climb onto the higher roof and explore!"

"Not roof. Dais. E.R.B. calls big platforms a dais."

"Dais. Got it." I vaulted up. It sounded regal, like a place for a throne or something. But it was just

7

a hot stretch of tarred roof out of the willow's shade, with metal pipe vents sticking up. And it took me right back to ordinary Main Street and civilization on the other side of the building.

I crouched low and stared over the edge. Ordinary people going about ordinary business. Ordinary shops all in a row: the card shop, the music shop, Woolworth's, Joe's Bar.

I leaned closer, staring at the man walking toward Joe's. It looked like—

It was him. Dad. I knew that plaid shirt, that slow easy walk. I knew the back of his head.

He paused outside the door of the bar, one hand in his pocket, the other lifting a cigarette to his mouth. My whole body tensed, watching, waiting. He wouldn't go in. He *couldn't.*

He looked handsome, standing there by the lamppost. These past two weeks, working that new job at a coffee shop, he'd been shaving, wearing neat clean clothes, combing his hair. Right now it was wavy, golden-brown in the sun. He always looked so good when he was working, when things were right.

He should be working right now. Two o'clock to ten o'clock, six days a week. He shouldn't be standin there on Main Street. He should *not* be outside Joe's Bar.

Two weeks. Things had been fine for two weeks. But two weeks was enough for one paycheck. And that was plenty for Joe's. I crouched in the shadows, as still and frozen as Sheeta, watching as he dropped the cigarette on the sidewalk, ground it out with his heel, and walked into Joe's.

8

I turned away. I didn't want to think about it. The prickles and tingles of jungle fever oozed out of me like air from a leaky balloon. I felt shaky. I had to get off the boma and away from Main Street.

"Let's go. It's getting late." I moved away from the edge.

Heather squinted up at the sky. "You're right. Kudu is getting low," she agreed in a low solemn voice. She hadn't noticed Joe's or Dad's. "Tomorrow we can come straight from school. We'll have more time. We can bring supplies."

She talked and planned while we climbed back across the limb into the willow. I was thinking about Dad. About whether he still had a job. About what Mom would do when he came home drunk. About how this time was supposed to be different.

I was thinking hard about Dad, not about the ladies in the banquet room. Not about melting into the shadows of the tree, like Sheeta. I wasn't using jungle cunning. And that was why my shirt caught on a rough piece of bark, spiking the shirt and me to the tree, right in front of the big picture window.

There were *lots* of women eating in there now. A fat lady was sitting at the table next to the window. My breath stuck in my throat.

"Help!" I whispered, desperate. My heart was banging so hard against the trunk, it sounded like a woodpecker.

The fat lady moved a big piece of cake toward her mouth. The cake went in, her eyes turned toward the window, and her fork fell to the plate.

She half-stood, eyes wide. I hugged the tree for

dear life with one arm, while my other arm gave a last desperate yank on my shirt. It ripped free.

"Waiter!"

But I didn't stay around to hear any more.

"Down, fast. We've been seen!"

Not even Tarzan could have got down the bole any faster. I lost some of my hair on one branch and part of the skin on my palm on another.

"What can they do?"

"We were trespassing. They could call the police!" Heather grabbed my arm. "Come on!"

"They don't own the tree!"

"No time to argue! Run for it!"

We cut through a driveway to Main Street and kept running, past all the shoppers and stores. I had a stitch in my side by the time we stopped at Third and High.

Heather said, panting, "We can still go back. This won't stop us. We . . . just . . . have to . . . do it . . . sneakier. Tomorrow." And she turned to head home, walking.

I kept running. Like Bara, the deer. Trying to outrun the dangers. All the dangers in the banquet room and the one big danger in Joe's Bar.

I wished I'd never climbed up on the dais. I wished I'd never seen Joe's. I wished I could stop thinking about what would happen at home tonight.

Two

□□□

The house smelled like spaghetti when I walked in. There was a pot of water boiling away and another pot of sauce, spitting red tomato bubbles all over the stove.

Spaghetti again. Whatever the tenth grade home economics class at Wilson High learned to fix, the Callahan family ate for days and days. Last week was tuna casserole.

"Geri! Water's boiling!" I yelled into the living room. But only Katie was in there, watching TV with her blanket snuggled up beside her. Some five-year-old baby.

I started down the hall, toward the bedrooms. "Water's boiling," I yelled again. "And the spaghetti sauce needs a lid."

Geri lay stretched out on her bed, staring up at the ceiling like it was a very fascinating movie. I craned my neck and stared too.

"What are you looking at?"

She said in a very slow calm voice, "I am releasing my inhibitions."

Geri's high school is two miles away. Whenever she misses the bus and has to walk home, she sacks

11

out on her bed to release her inhibitions. Anyone else would say, "I'm tired," or "I'm beat." Not Geri.

Once I looked up inhibitions in the dictionary. It didn't have a thing to do with sore feet. She just liked to sound wise and dramatic, lying there with her frizzy brown hair spread out all over the pillow, and her stack of singles going around and around on the record player.

I kicked her notebook out of my way. "I'll put the lid on for you," I said, feeling generous. If Geri was late, it didn't matter that I was late.

"Thanks, Erin. You're really a big help, Erin." And she focused on her ceiling dots again.

I heard the click of high heels on the sidewalk. Mom, walking home from the bus stop. I knew it even before I looked out the window. No one else had her brisk, firm click.

I watched her coming up the driveway. No one else walked so straight and proud, or looked quite so dignified and businesslike in blazers and skirts and heels. Her secretary clothes.

"Erin, how did school go today?" Her arm went around my shoulders for a quick hug, before she moved around the kitchen, clearing the table, tending to the pots, and going out to the service porch to dump a load in the washing machine.

"Fine." I bit my lip, thinking about Dad.

"Where's Geri?"

I jerked my thumb toward the bedroom. "Releasing her inhibitions."

Mom grinned. "Have a hard day, Geri?" she called down the hall.

Geri appeared in the doorway a few seconds later.

"I've been practicing my poem for speech class," she announced. She put one hand over her heart and made her voice low and breathy.

"And the highwayman came riding—
Riding—riding—
The highwayman came riding, up to the old
    inn-door."

Geri threw her head back, striding into the kitchen. "Then look for me by moonlight," she hissed. "Watch for me by moonlight. I'll come to thee by moonlight . . ." She threw the spaghetti into the colander, without breaking rhythm. ". . . though *Hell* should bar the way!"

"Not that one," Katie whimpered. "That's the bloody one. Do the itchy one."

I giggled.

"Not itchy, Katie," Geri grinned. *"Gitche."* She straightened, holding the Parmesan cheese container like a torch.

"By the shores of Gitche Gumee
By the Shining Big-Sea-Water. . . ."

Geri is the biggest ham on earth. She should have joined the drama club. And she would have, if she didn't always have to be home right after school; if it weren't for—him.

I swallowed hard. If Mom only knew, she

13

wouldn't be clowning around, pretending to find the "off" button on Geri, laughing as she handed me a stack of plates.

"Here, Erin, set the table, while I change clothes."

It was hard to fit four plates around the little kitchen table. We used to eat at the dining room table. But it was gone one day when I came home from school. I didn't have to ask what happened to it. The same thing that happened to a lot of other things, like the silver service and some of Mom's jewelry. They'd been sold, to make up for all the money that got spent at places like Joe's Bar. To pay debts. The car didn't disappear that way, though. Dad totaled it in a crash last year.

Mom sat down with a big long sigh. "Are you tired after running two thousand miles?" she asked herself in a teasing voice that covered up the tiredness. When Mom changed out of her work clothes, it seemed like she hung her whole work self up on the hanger. In the old pants and shirt she was wearing now, the briskness and the pep were gone. She looked beat.

I was glad she didn't know yet that Dad's new job was gone, like the table. Maybe, just maybe he'd stay out all night. Maybe he wouldn't come back until I was in bed. And our evening would be calm and relaxed, like now.

Mom pushed back Katie's long stringy bangs. "Aren't you hungry, honey? You're just picking at your food."

14

"I'm eating," Katie mumbled, pushing her onions to the edge of her plate.

A loud rumble sounded from the service porch, followed by ker-splat, ker-splat, ker-splat.

Mom nodded toward the noise. "Keep going, Matilda, old girl," she called.

Matilda was practically an antique. She didn't have a permanent press cycle or any of the other settings that most washing machines did. She only washed one way, and that way took her practically across the room, jiggling and vibrating. That was how she got her name, from the song "Waltzing Matilda." Mom and Geri always patted her on the lid and told her how terrific she was, with each new load. And it worked—so far.

"I made a new dessert," Geri said, over the ker-splats.

"Dessert?" Katie's face lit up. She was done separating onions; now she was working on the green pepper pieces.

"Brownies. Only I'm not having one. I'm on a diet." Geri held the plate away from herself heroically.

They were brownie bricks.

"These sure are good, Geri," I said, scrunching my face to crack down for another bite. "It's a good thing none of us has dentures."

"I followed the recipe." Geri stared at the plate forlornly.

Katie tried to pull out the walnuts, then gave up. "Can I have an egg, please?"

15

Mom got up without a word and came back with a hard boiled egg. Katie ended up with an egg almost every night. But Mom still tried to encourage her to eat what we did, so every night she fooled around with the food on her plate, before she got her egg.

Mrs. Morris next door babysat Katie after kindergarten, and she said all Katie ate for lunch was bologna. It probably hurt Mrs. Morris's feelings. Cooking and gardening were her big things in life. She sometimes brought us samples of her desserts or hot dishes.

"Doug and I can't possibly eat all this," she'd say in her soft voice to Mom. As if we were doing *her* a favor by eating it.

But her casseroles always had things like mushrooms or pimentos or broccoli in them. And even her cakes and cookies sometimes had flecks of green zucchini or orange carrots inside. Katie probably figured she was safe only with bologna. No wonder she was so skinny and mousy looking all the time.

The door slammed in the living room. My whole body tensed. I tried to concentrate on my brownie. But instead, my eyes focused past the kitchen doorway, into the living room.

He was stumbling across the room, grabbing the wall, then the table for support. His face was red, loose. He was mumbling. A moment later I heard a thud. He'd found the couch.

Katie stopped eating her egg and stared down at the table. I looked at Geri. Geri looked at Mom.

For a split second, Mom's body sagged in the chair. But the next instant her mouth tightened. Her face got hard. "Damn," she muttered. She pushed her chair back and stood up, straight and tall, and headed toward the noise.

"I'll dry the dishes later, Geri," I called, heading for my bedroom. I wanted to be in my room when the shouting started.

"Take Katie; help her get ready for bed," she yelled back. I pretended not to hear. Katie always crawled under her bed when I tried to help.

The best thing about my room, besides being just mine, was the trapdoor in the closet. It led to the attic. I always kept a chair in the closet, to climb up. I'd practiced so much, that now I could get up without making a sound. There wasn't any floor up there, just rafters with insulation in-between, and one light bulb, with a pull chain. I had laid a little board under the light. I settled down on it now, with my notebook and pen. The attic and the notebook was Bal-Za's territory.

No one but me knew about Bal-Za. I made her up. Her name, her story, even her secret identity. That was the best part of the story, and a deeply guarded secret. In all of E.R.B.'s books, Tarzan just had a son, Korak. But in my story, Tarzan had a daughter. Bal-Za. She was strong and brave, like her father, and pretty, with long blond hair that earned her the name Bal-Za. Bal for golden; Za for girl. I hadn't told a soul about Bal-Za. Not even Heather.

I had worked out Bal-Za's history in the attic

17

one night last month, writing under the light bulb until ten o'clock. It was as exciting as any of E.R.B.'s books.

Bal-Za had been kidnapped by evil people who hated Tarzan. Her captors brought her to a hidden lost kingdom deep in the jungle. Azumba. I could picture Azumba so clearly. It looked like the Mayan ruins I had seen in schoolbooks, with big carved statues, stone temples for strange gods, and surrounded by jungle.

I figured that Bal-Za had been about Katie's age when she was kidnapped. Now she was twelve. She didn't remember who her real parents were. She didn't know that the famous Tarzan was her father. She had spent most of her life in the heavy dark buildings of Azumba.

But she knew that she was not like the others in the city. They were dark-skinned, and she was fair-skinned and blond. Her captors told her that her parents lived far away, and that she would be kept prisoner until she reached fourteen. Then she would be sacrificed to the gods.

Bal-Za has decided to try and escape into the jungle, to search for her real people, to find out who she is. . . .

That was the part where I left off. It was a great story. Bal-Za had great adventures in store for her. She was a real heroine, brave and beautiful.

"You're right you won't!" Mom's voice rose up to the rafters in cold fury.

18

"Who do you think you are?" Loud, surly, slurred.

"I'm the idiot who pays your bills. But no more. I told you not to come back this way!"

I tried to blank out the fighting and the curses and turn back to my notebook, back to the story feeling, the jungle and ancient temples.

"Get the hell out, you drunken fool. And don't come back."

I wrote fast, hard; it was a blur of words that didn't make sense.

After one last "Get Out!" the shouting stopped. Then came a mighty door-slam that shook the house right up to my attic. Then—quiet.

Deadly quiet. I chewed my pen and stared up at the light bulb. Deadly quiet in the house, the attic, and in the sacred city of Azumba, where Bal-Za waited in hiding. I wrapped my arms around my knees hard to tighten my whole body against the trembly sick feeling.

The fight's over, Erin. Dad's gone—for now. Think about other things. Like Bal-Za. Like the boma. I hugged my knees harder, squeezed my eyes shut, and tried to bring back the happy feeling of this afternoon and our discovery.

I couldn't wait to go back. We'd be as silent as Histah, the snake, wriggling up the bole of the willow. Window or no window, we'd reach the roof unseen. We'd brave the dangers with skill and cunning. Like Bal-Za, cloaked and hooded, moving

19

slowly through the dark streets of Azumba by night. Learning the guard posts, learning the layout, planning her escape.

I finished the sentence with a shaky curlicue that went round and round; then I opened the attic hatch and started down.

Three

□□□

Heather opened her backpack after school the next day with a big smug grin.

"Look what I brought." Inside were a hammer, long nails, and an old splintery board.

"What's it all for?"

"A step. For the boma tree." She tossed her head, flipping back her thick blond hair. "Then we can get up to the roof quick, without all that shinnying."

It was a great idea, if we could manage to get the step nailed up without falling into the alley or toppling into the river. We moved slowly, stealthily down Main Street, through the narrow driveway, and down the back alley, to our willow.

"We tried to make a step like this at camp," Heather said, pulling herself into the tree.

"Did it work?"

"The counselor made us stop. Too bad, too. Camp Firefly has tons of tall trees that don't have low branches. Anyway, that's how I got the idea of putting the step up here." She balanced against the crotch and stuck some nails in her mouth.

"Thought . . . about it . . . all night," she mumbled through a mouthful of nails. But the first nail

21

bent when she banged, the second fell down to the alley, and on the third try, her whole hand slipped.

"I've got a better idea." I scooted up behind, so that we were almost wedged together in the crotch. "You hold the board; I'll pound over your shoulder."

It was hard to get force behind the hammer swings because I had to reach so far. My shoulders started hurting right away. And with each bang, my eyes shot toward the window, checking. Good thing there wasn't a tea party going on today.

"Careful!" Heather hissed, each time I raised the hammer. One bang came almost to her thumbnail. She jerked back; we both swayed.

"I said *be careful!* That's the only right thumb I've got!"

"I *am* being careful! Duck your head so I can reach better."

Five nails later, one finally went in far enough to secure a corner of the board. Between us, we got six out of the next thirteen nails in.

"Up, up, hurry!" I felt panicky. Any second some waiter would wander into the banquet room and catch us.

The step worked perfectly. Even Sheeta couldn't have gotten up the bole as quickly and quietly as we did.

The roof was warm from Kudu's rays slanting in through the leafy branches. I dropped down near the edge and let the greenness and warmth soak into me. When I peered down over the edge, the jungle fever broke out in goose bumps on my arms. This was more than just the edge of a roof. It was the edge

22

of something else, unseen, powerful, separating us from the world below. We had climbed into a spell; the spell of the boma.

Heather's voice pulled me back to practical everyday matters. "I brought us a snack."

I stared. "Beef jerky!"

"It was the most authentic thing I could find at the candy counter." She pulled it out in long stringy pieces.

"It's the opposite of authentic." I ripped the strings with my teeth. "Tarzan ate things raw, not dried-out and salty and—" I yanked, "tough." We grinned at each other.

Heather stretched out with a contented sigh. "I found a new word for the cipher. 'Tarmangani.' "

"What does it mean?"

"Well." She rested her chin in her hands. "Denizens are people with trained jungle senses, like us, right? Tarmanganis are the opposite. The civilized slobs. Like the people in the restaurant."

"Tarmangani: un-denizen." I wrote it down in the cipher. "I found a word, too. 'Goro.' Means moon."

"That's an important one. Let's get it down."

I rolled over and stared up at the white clouds and blue sky. How would Goro look from the boma, with the black night all around?

"I wish we could stay up here long enough to see it. Goro, I mean," I said, wishing out loud.

The idea slid lazily through my head. Goro, the stars, the dark, the boma— I pulled in my knees and sat up in one big spin.

23

"Heather, what if—what if we *could* stay when it gets dark? Even all night?"

"That's crazy. We can't just disappear all night. No one would let us come in the day, if they knew."

We each had our own excuses. Her mom thought she stayed for after-school sports. I gave Geri all sorts of excuses, whatever popped into my head.

"Of course they wouldn't let us—if they knew. But . . ." My mind raced ahead, pulling the idea out of the fog. "What if your mom thought you were spending the night with me, and *my* mom thought I was spending the night with you?"

Her eyes gleamed, catlike. "It'd be just like at camp! But no counselors. Just us!"

"And more jungly!"

"We'd need flashlights."

"And food. And blankets, or sleeping bags."

"We could do it on the last day of school. Our own party." Then she shook her head. "No, not party. That's the wrong word. Ritual." She made her voice low and dramatic. "A boma ritual, far above the banks of the Histah River. To initiate our boma."

She made it sound almost sacred.

"It'll be our initiation, too," I said, getting more and more excited. "Our survival initiation, to prove that we're true denizens. Just like Tarzan and Korak proved themselves in the jungle."

"He killed his own meat with his bare hands."

"What can we kill?"

She held up the rest of her jerky with a giggle. "The sacred cow!"

24

Four

◻◻◻

"**B**est idea you ever had. It'll be as good as camp. Better. Just us and Goro and the boma!" Heather chattered, while I raced the shopping cart up and down the aisles of the Corner Mart, throwing in the things on Geri's list. Milk, bread, canned vegetables. . . .

I was a little worried. We'd stayed too long at the boma. Geri needed the groceries to start dinner. She'd really be mad.

"For our ritual we have to choose supplies carefully," Heather said.

"Yeah. Potato chips, cookies—"

"No. Not that kind of stuff. We have to be authentic." It was her loud, stubborn voice. I had a feeling I was going to get tired of that word before too long.

"And we'll need tools. And our E.R.B. books. And—" her voice got slow and thoughtful, "we need the right clothes."

I looked up suspiciously.

"What do you mean, the right clothes?"

"At initiations people usually wear special outfits. Like costumes, almost. We'll need one like Korak or Tarzan would wear. Or any denizen."

25

"And just where are we going to get an animal fur? From the local leopard, maybe?"

"Across the street." She said it so matter-of-factly, I half-expected to see a leopard standing right there. But it was only the thrift shop, with cracked shabby paint and streaked windows.

"What's that place got to do with denizens?"

"They've got all kinds of cheap junk. Mom always gets stuff for Halloween costumes there. We can at least look."

"But I have to get home!" Mom wouldn't like me shopping in there, anyway. It was strange that Heather's mom, who had plenty of money, bought used bargains all over the place, and my mom, who just barely had enough for groceries, would shudder to pick out *anything* in a place like this.

"It'll only take a minute to check. Come on."

The place smelled like an old musty closet. Racks and racks of wrinkled, tired-looking clothes, bins of cheap jewelry, shelves of ratty shoes.

"How much money have you got?" Heather whispered.

"Seventy-five cents, not counting grocery change."

"I've got a dollar. We ought to be able to find *something*."

The good coats were way out of our budget, even in a place like this. But some of the ones that were really bad, with the lining hanging on the floor and big matted spots in the fur, were just about affordable. Then I saw it.

Big black spots on a sleek gold, furry background. A burnt place in the back, and a broken zipper. All for a dollar twenty-five. Size eighteen, so there was plenty of material.

"Come on, let's take it and get out of here." I was really late. And this place was so dirty and decrepit, from the dingy furniture to the basket of junky jewelry by the cash register. Who'd ever want a string of pearls with the pearl coating off, or a dirty white pompon Santa Claus pin, or— My eyes stopped at a big round green badge near the side of the basket.

There was a leprechaun perched on a pot of gold at the top of the badge and the words "Erin Go Bragh" printed across the bottom.

Erin Go Bragh. Ireland Forever. Most people just used those words on St. Patrick's Day. But they meant something else to me. Dad used to call me that all the time when I was little.

"Here comes Erin Go Bragh, coming in for a landing!" he'd yell, swooping me around like an airplane, my arms straight out. Or, grabbing me by my feet: "Here's Erin Go Bragh, folks. Now where's that Blarney Stone?"

I thought Go Bragh was my middle name until I reached kindergarten. Even now, he called me that sometimes, if he was in a good mood, if he was . . . okay.

"Will that be all, girls?" The shop lady smiled a big smile that showed black teeth toward the back. She leaned toward us over the counter, like she was sharing a secret, and dropped her voice. "I remember when I used to dress up, too. I wore old gowns and coats just like that one."

I looked up, indignant. But Heather answered.

"Actually," she said in a low, husky voice, "we wanted to slay our own leopard for the skin. We would have slit the jugular vein. But there aren't any around, except in the zoo." She dropped her voice to a whisper. "And they're protected."

We left the store, heads high. Heather bragged for two blocks.

"Did you see her face? I bet *nobody* ever said a thing like that to her before!"

"Dress-up. *Dress-up!* Do we look like six year olds or something?"

At the corner of Third and High, I pulled out my school scissors. They weren't meant for cutting through coats. But with one of us cutting, and the other pulling and ripping, the old fur finally gave in.

"Now remember," Heather said, stuffing her half in her backpack, "find just the right time to ask your mom. She *has* to say yes."

"You too." But then a new thought came to me. A thought that stuck my feet to the sidewalk.

"Heather—if you ask to spend the night at my house, will your mom mind about"—I swallowed and forced the words out—"mind about my dad?" I felt my face get hot. It was hard to talk about him. Even to Heather, my best friend.

She knew it was hard. I could tell by the way she looked down for just a second and bit her lip. "I

28

didn't think about that. I don't know. I never asked before, you know—" Her voice trailed off.

She was right. And *he* was the reason why I'd never asked her over for the night; why Mom didn't let us have any friends overnight. And, of course, Mrs. Prescott knew about him. Everybody knew. After all, he didn't work most of the time, and he stumbled up and down the block, back and forth from Joe's, where everyone could see.

"Don't worry, Erin." Heather tossed her hair back in her confident, assured way. "I'll think of something, if she does . . . mind. And she won't, anyway, because she likes you and your mom and all." Her voice drifted off, as she started down her street.

I jogged the rest of the way home, with my grocery bag and leopard skin bumping up and down on my arm. I didn't want even to think about how late it was. Might even be dinnertime already. And no groceries.

But when I turned the corner onto our street and saw the smoke coming out of the chimney, I knew I had other things to worry about than being late when I got home.

Five

◨◨◨

High hot flames in the fireplace, Gallo wine bottles on the table, and *him* on the couch. I knew how it would be even before I opened the door. After all, who in their right mind, in their *sober* mind, would start a roaring fire on a perfectly warm day? Even in Wisconsin you don't need a fire going in *May*.

But the weather didn't matter to him. He got absolutely fascinated with the fire. Like now, lying there watching the flames, his face loose, his eyes red.

So yesterday ended the new job and the neat clothes. Things were bad again, like before. I hugged my grocery bag tight and hurried across the liquor-smelly oven of a living room. He smiled blankly at me. He mumbled something too, but I kept walking. I didn't want to look in the fireplace to see what was burning. Last time he threw in good lumber from the garage. The time before that, it was the toybox. The pile of winter firewood had gone up in smoke a long time ago.

The phone cord stretched across the kitchen and out through the partly opened back door. How to find Geri: follow the phone cord.

She was sitting on the back porch railing, talking in a low voice, while Katie rode her training wheel bike down the driveway. When Geri looked up and saw me, her expression changed to a scowl.

"Gotta go, Karen," she muttered into the receiver. "My sister's finally here with the groceries."

Her voice wasn't so soft back in the kitchen.

"What took you so long! I *need* these groceries to fix dinner, you know!"

She looked hot. And mad. She'd probably been stuck here since she got home from school, making sure the house didn't burn down.

I felt weird. The happy excitement of our boma plans was still floating around somewhere in the back of my head. But in the front part, some tight tense knot was pounding. Evil smelly tarmangani.

The weird feeling spilled out in craziness.

"Here's your groceries, bossy." I pulled out a can of green beans, set it on the floor, and rolled it across the kitchen. Next came the applesauce.

"*Stop it!*"

I straightened up holding a kidney bean can. Usually Geri was a pretty good sport. She didn't get screaming mad very often.

"When are you going to grow up, Erin?" she asked in a low angry voice. "When are you going to start helping around here?"

"I bought the groceries." I could make my voice low and angry, too. Suddenly it was her I was mad at. "I have to get them almost every day, you know. *And* walk to school with Katie in the morning. And dry dishes. And. . . ."

"Shut up." She pulled out a pan and slammed

31

the cupboard shut. "Go play with Katie. That's about your level."

If I'd had a can in my hand just then, it would have gone sailing through the air. Instead, I slammed the door as hard as I could and escaped to the backyard.

Dinner was overdone hamburger patties. Mom hardly touched her food. When she glanced toward the living room, her lips pressed together tightly, and her eyes smoldered like the hot coals in the fireplace. She took a deep breath and turned back to us.

"How did school go today?" she asked, pushing back her half-full plate. Same question she asked every night at dinner. But tonight her voice was tight, forced.

"Erin, how was your day?" The proud look in her eyes and the firm set to her jaw said the rest: "Come on, don't let him wreck everything. We'll talk, anyway. Try."

I fiddled with my fork. "Fine." The next few words came out on their own. "Uh—Heather and I want to, uh, celebrate the last day of school next Thursday. She wants to know if I can, uh, spend the night." It wasn't a lie.

"Fine," said Mom in the same too calm, detached voice that meant she was covering up very different feelings. "Walk over while it's still light, though. I can't get you over after dark without a car. I don't like you walking alone in the dark."

Perfect. Couldn't be better. I felt a little guilty about the triumphant thrill that shot through me.

Geri sat back with a big groan. "I wish spending

the night at someone's house was all I had to worry about. I think my teachers sit up nights thinking up new tortures. I have three finals and two term papers due next week!"

"Just take it as it comes," Mom said. "One thing at a time." Mom's famous last words. Even tonight, with that grim tight look on her face, the words came out automatically.

"Katie—" Mom turned toward Katie's chair and stopped. It was empty. Quiet, mousy Katie had slipped away without anyone even noticing.

"All right, this is the last time I'm going to tell you," said a small voice from the dining room. I looked through the doorway. Katie was sitting on the floor, playing with her dollhouse. She held the mother doll up to face the father doll.

"You leave that bottle alone, you hear?" she said in a stern little whisper. "You're drinking too much milk! You'll have to go live someplace else if you don't shape up."

A nervous giggle slid up my throat. Geri giggled too. Mom shook her head. "Good Lord," she said. Then she laughed too. But it was a short bitter laugh. And the look she shot toward the living room was not one bit amused. I'd better be in my room when the fight started.

It was very hot in the attic. Sweat trickled down my forehead as I hunched over my notebook. But I couldn't leave. Things were happening to Bal-Za; they had to be told. More and more memories were stirring inside her head and turning into haunting dreams at night. Of a place before Azumba. Of faces: a woman's, kind and pretty, and a man's, strong, rugged, handsome. She had to find out what those memories meant. It all had to do with who she was, and why she was here in his hidden jungle city.

I could picture her crouching against the old temple, her long golden hair falling over her shoulders, her eyes tightly shut, as she tried desperately to remember. Her memories of a strong, kind father were so long ago, so vague in her mind. If she could only remember more. If she could somehow find that place again. . . .

Six

□□□

I woke up late the next morning with a stuffy nose and scratchy throat.

"Stay home if you don't feel well," Mom said.

I stayed in bed. I intended to get up. There were important things to do after school. I couldn't let a little cold interfere with our plans. Katie and Geri and Mom all got dressed and left, and I was still thinking about getting up. I could hear the radio going in the kitchen and cupboards creaking open and shut. Then footsteps moved down the hall, and Dad stood in the doorway. His clothes were rumpled and he wasn't shaved, but his eyes were okay. He'd slept it off.

"How about an egg, Erin?"

"No. I'm not hungry," I said sullenly.

"You'll feel better if you eat," he went on in a loud voice, paying no attention to my words. That's the way he always acts when one of us is sick. Loud, bossy, sure of what's best. When Geri had her appendix out a few years ago, Dad was the only one who could coax her out of bed when her stitches hurt. He was just as stubborn and determined as she was, and he kept on talking and arguing right over her groans and moans.

Sure enough, my egg came in on a tray ten minutes later. It was poached, on toast, and there was a napkin and a glass of milk beside it.

"How's that? Not bad for your old dad, eh?" He sounded pleased as punch. I had to nod.

"Yeah, it looks good." I wasn't hungry, but because he was watching, waiting for me to take a bite, I lifted my spoon.

"That's the way. That'll make you feel better."

He stood by the wall, relaxed, cheerful, his fingers tapping the dresser top. He could make it sound like an instrument, the way he flicked his fingers fast, one after another, against the wood.

He saw me watching his fingers. "What about this one, Erin? Remember this?" He snapped the fingers of his right hand, then his left, then whacked his left fist into his right palm. Snap, snap, clap. Snap, snap, clap. Done fast, it sounded like a castanet. When he first tried to teach me, back when I was about seven, I spent days walking around the house, counting and snapping, trying to remember what hand went when. One-two-three. Snap-snap-clap. And I'd finally mastered it.

I hesitated a minute, then pushed the tray back and lifted my hands slowly. Snap, snap, clap. Snap, snap, clap. My fingers had a good memory. The rhythm was automatic, even now. I could feel the grin stretch across my face, slow, grudging almost.

He joined in. Snap, snap, clap. Snap, snap, clap. Steady and rhythmic. "Not bad, not bad." He gave an approving nod, then leaned back against the dresser.

"Erin Go Bragh . . ." His voice was slow, thoughtful. "You're growing up, you know that?" He shook his head. "All you girls are. Too fast." Still shaking his head, he left the room.

I pulled the tray back in place. But I couldn't eat. The egg was cold. And there was a funny hollow feeling in my stomach.

It had been a long time since he taught me that finger trick; a long time since those airplane rides and the days when he was always like this morning, always okay, clear-eyed, in charge. I could only vaguely remember it.

There had not been the red-eyed, red-faced, smelly person living inside him, then. No bottles around and no fires. The whole family did things together then. And he had a regular job, an important job, not like these coffee shops and restaurant ones for a few weeks at a time.

I pushed back the covers. Got dressed, made the bed, straightened the room. Much better not to think about him at all; not to let the half-memories wash over me like a rush of homesickness. A little cold was no reason to stay home anyway. Much better to get back to school, to Heather, and the boma.

At the kitchen doorway, I stopped and stared.

Dad was cooking. There were hard boiled eggs all over the counter, most of them shelled and split in half, and minus a yolk. He was dumping some tuna out of its can into a bowl with one hand and puffing on a cigarette with the other. The breakfast dishes had been piled into a high dirty heap in the sink. He was wearing Mom's apron over his dirty shirt.

"Dad . . . what are you doing?"

"Dinner." He sounded very pleased with himself. "I'm helping out today."

I stared as he mixed the tuna with mayonnaise, then stuffed the mixture into the egg-white cups. I'd never heard of tuna deviled eggs before.

"What happened to the yolks?"

"I threw them down the garbage disposal." He took another drag on his cigarette, while he plopped in more tuna. "Don't need them. This is more creative."

Poor Katie. Those were her week's dinner rations. Tuna deviled eggs for dinner.

"Dad, you better save one plain egg for Katie. She won't eat tuna."

"I know. I know." But his hand was waving me away, and he was concentrating on unclogging the paprika bottle. It came out in a big red clump, smothering two eggs.

Dad in the morning was another kind of dad. The picture of him standing there in Mom's apron, with shirtsleeves rolled up and a cigarette in his hand stayed in my mind all the way to school. And him serving me breakfast on a tray, all proper, with a napkin and everything. And his proud, pleased smile. It was almost like he was trying to make up for last night. . . .

I shook the thought away, almost angrily. By the

time I got home this afternoon, he'd have found some money, somehow, and gone to Joe's.

Morning recess was still going on when I reached school. Heather ran to meet me at the gate.

"Erin! Guess what? Mom said okay to the overnight!" She lowered her voice. "I guess she figured things were okay at your house, or your mom wouldn't have let you invite me."

Things were not okay at my house. Things were hardly ever okay at my house. But I didn't want to think about that. I'd think about the boma instead. And our ritual. It *was* going to happen. Just one more week to go.

Seven

◻◻◻

The next week was a big wheel rolling toward Thursday, the last day of school. We went to the boma every day to stash supplies for the overnight. Up on the warm sunny roof, it didn't matter so much that things were worse at home, that the fires were roaring in the fireplace every day. From the boma heights, only our ritual mattered. We sewed leopard skins, made all the arrangements, and prayed that the good weather would hold.

It should have stayed warm. After all, early June is practically summer. But in Wisconsin, warm weather isn't ever a sure thing. Late Wednesday, the low gloomy clouds started to roll in. By Thursday afternoon, they were low enough to spray mist on us, as we walked to the boma.

Heather was happy about the weather. "Camouflage," she said with a satisfied nod, as we turned down the alley. "No one will be able to see us. It's even mistier here by the river! It'll hide us getting the heavy packs up."

It *was* clumsy, getting my big overnight case up the willow. I felt more like Tantor, the elephant, than sleek Sheeta, hoisting it up the bole, then down with a thud on the boma roof.

"Made it."

"Yeah."

And then we stood there for a minute, looking at each other. In the quiet and the fog, the jungle fever started to change to something else—something solemn and heavy, like the mist. I could feel it in the prickles on my skin, in the look on Heather's face, as she reached into her bag for her leopard skin, in the foggy air, still thickening over the river.

Our plan was working. Tonight we would disappear from civilization. No sisters, no parents, no beds or tables or TVs. Just the boma and us.

We put on the leopard skins. Heather tied hers like a baggy apron over her brown sweater and jeans. Mine went on like a big poncho. On the ground, with all the everyday things around us, the leopard skins would have looked ridiculous. Here, their weirdness held dignity and majesty.

Heather felt it, too. "You look—different," she said, staring. "Almost really . . . wild."

The fog muffled the usual street noises. Cars driving past the other side of the building sounded very far away. We were alone, padding about, tying our rope to the tree limb and the roof vent, and draping the tablecloth over it to make a flimsy tent cover. Then, just sitting by the roof's edge, waiting. . . .

The spell was fragile. I was afraid to talk; glad to hear Heather's voice, low and solemn:

41

"We should start with E.R.B. It's only right."

I brought *Son of Tarzan,* my favorite, in honor of the occasion. I opened to the place where Korak had to fight the great Numa, fending off the tearing claws, the great teeth, the powerful muscles, until his knife found the cat's jugular vein, again and again.

It was so clear, so real. When a howl rose up from somewhere below, I jumped and almost sent my book off the edge.

"What was that!"

Heather stared down. "Zwumba," she whispered. I hadn't heard that one before. It was her own word. A mystery name for the howl coming out of the fog. I nodded.

"Zwumba is hungry."

"So am I." The munchies that were stashed away in the packs sounded wonderful all of a sudden.

"Wait." She held out a hand. Her eyebrows came together in a frown. "I was thinking. This is our survival initiation, right? We shouldn't be able to grab just any old thing all packaged up and ready to eat, right? Fritos and candy bars and all that."

I sighed. I thought I'd talked her out of all that "authentic" food. "What are we going to do, stalk the Zwumba?"

"No, but I was thinking about it, yesterday. I went to the market . . ." She gave me a nervous look, "to see what sort of food would come closest to the right stuff and. . . ." She pulled an insulated container out of her bookbag.

I stared at the carton suspiciously.

"Well . . ." She gave me another quick look,

then reached down to unzip the container. We both looked down at . . . liver. Slices of red-brown, slimy, slippery, awful raw liver all heaped on top of each other like fat ugly snakes.

"What did you have to go and get *that* stuff for! I can't eat that! I'll barf."

"You said not to get any more jerky! Anyway, this is raw. Just like what Tarzan and Korak ate. It was lots cheaper than anything else. And this is an initiation, remember, not a party." But her mouth twisted strangely too, when she looked down at her wriggly mass.

Raw liver. When just a few yards away were Fritos and potato chips, candy bars, crackers. I swallowed. I thought of the chapter I had just finished, of the tearing claws, the warm, bloody flesh.

She was right. Drat her for bringing it, but it had to be the liver.

I felt like gagging when she reached into the carton and pulled out a long, slithery, snake-shaped piece. "Histah meat." My voice sounded choked.

She nodded. "From the dark waters below." That was where it belonged. The stuff slipped out of my fingers when I reached for it. It fell on the tarred roof. When I picked it back up with my thumb and forefinger, little pebbles and dirt pieces stuck to the back. With a little shudder I dropped it again and grasped another slippery piece.

"Well," Heather said. Was it the misty haze that gave her face that green-yellow color? "Well . . ." and she took a bite.

I couldn't watch. If I did, it would be all over

43

with my stomach. I turned my head. When I looked back, she was sitting very still. Her face was even more green. Her eyes were kind of glassy. And her Histah meat was gone.

"You . . . finished it?" I shuddered, asking. She nodded. For a brief instant, I hated her for going through with it. Because now I had to.

If I wasted time thinking about it, I'd lose my nerve. I made like a robot. My mouth opened, the cold slippery stuff went in, my mouth shut. But when I reached the part where my teeth were supposed to take over and attack the slimy mass, the robot malfunctioned. I ran over to the roof's edge.

In another second, Heather was there too, leaning over. I hoped there weren't any innocent people emptying trash in the alley below. The Histah meat had returned to the dark waters below.

I felt trembly and headachy, afterwards. There was a horrible leftover slimy taste in my mouth. I would never eat again.

"Worst idea I had in my whole life," Heather moaned. "The other stuff I brought isn't so bad. Bananas, nuts."

I put my hand on her mouth. "Don't talk about food right now."

I brought out the cipher. At the end of the last column I wrote: "Zwumba—mysterious howling river beast," and then "Bwarf—raw Histah meat. Inedible." And shut the book with a bang.

June days are long. But with Kudu hidden behind low clouds, the nighttime feeling came on fast. The fog rose with the night like a white ghost animal

44

with long curling arms, reaching up to our boma, wrapping around us.

We huddled under the tablecloth tent in our sweaters and leopard skins. Heather pulled her end of the blanket all the way up to her ears. In the glow of the flashlight she really did look like a wild girl.

"No matter the cold, the wet," she whispered, teeth chattering, "we can endure it."

"And after tonight," I added solemnly, "we'll be initiated together. Like sisters. Sisters of the Secret Cipher."

Heather stared back, all eyes in the fog.

"Sisters of the Secret Cipher! Great idea! We'll need secret names, too! Mine will be ..." She chewed her lip, thinking. "I know! Sabora. After the she-lion."

"Mine will be Za." Bal-Za had the rest of the name, but I didn't tell her that. There were some things that even secret sisters couldn't share.

"Za it is, then. We will guard our secrets, our code, our names."

"We will seal it in blood." In the jungle all is sealed in blood, after all.

Sabora brought out the knife. A quick tiny slash on the fingertip. A solemn oath: "We will tell no one of this boma, or of our sisterhood."

I turned off the flashlight and rubbed my throbbing finger. I tried to snuggle deeper into the blanket. My feet stuck out.

So, I could endure the cold, the bwarf, no pillow. Denizens grew stronger with hardships. So it would be with Sabora and Za.

45

Eight

◻◻◻

The next time I opened my eyes, it was impossible to see through the thick night. Why was the house so cold and dark? And what was that clicking noise?

Then I remembered. The boma. And the noise was Heather's teeth chattering.

What time was it? I peered out from under the tablecloth. The rest of the world had disappeared into the fog.

"Ugh." Heather rolled over, trying to pull my side of the blanket with her. She shone the flashlight on her watch.

"It's four thirty. And I'm so cold they could chop me into ice cubes."

"I'm starving."

She shone the light on the food bag. "There are bananas in there. And nuts."

Bananas. They sounded fantastic. We both had two.

Four forty.

I pushed my damp hair off my face. "No wonder Tarzan picked nice warm jungles."

"Two girls freeze to death on restaurant roof,"

46

Heather whispered mournfully. "I can see the head-lines already."

"What would Korak do? Or Tarzan?"

"Build a fire. Find someplace warm. Or suffer in noble silence."

A giggle slid up through my scratchy throat. "We're not doing any of those things. And after last night we're supposed to be true denizens."

"I'll be a true denizen when I thaw out."

I squinted up through the fog. "Can't even tell if Kudu's up. When do you think we should go down?"

"Six o'clock. Lots of people go to work then. It'd be safe. We can stop at my house first. Mom and Dad'll be sleeping upstairs. I'll fix cocoa." Her voice stopped on that last word, tasting it almost.

I could taste it, too. Hot, steamy, and chocolatey all the way down. "Cocoa. . . ."

"Oh, I can't stand it! Don't say it anymore."

"So what are we going to do until six?"

"Think about cocoa."

"No." I reached for my knapsack and pulled out two E.R.B. books. "Here." I plunked *Tarzan of the Apes* in front of her. We had started our ritual with E.R.B. We could end it that way, too. "If you think *we've* got it so hard, read about jungle Africa." If anyone could make us forget the cold and the damp, it was E.R.B.

I held my book hard, made my eyes focus on the words, wriggled my toes, flexed my muscles, blinked my eyes. When I checked my watch a while later, I

47

was sure the fog had wrecked it. Only five minutes had passed.

It was going to be a very long hour.

"*Za!*" Heather grabbed my arm.

"What!" There was danger below. The tree was falling down. The river was overflowing. "What's wrong!"

"It's not Africa!"

I shone my flashlight on her face. The initiation had been too much for her.

"Of course it's not Africa! It's Maddens roof, our boma!"

"No, I mean the book *Tarzan of the Apes.* Za, have you read this one clear through to the end? It's crazy. You won't believe it."

"Believe *what?*"

"Tarzan comes to *Wisconsin* to find Jane. To the Wisconsin north woods!" She waved the book at me. "Here, read it yourself. Start right here."

"You're kidding."

It sent a funny tingle through me, seeing the word Wisconsin at the top of the page of an E.R.B. book. Tarzan, searching for Jane, getting caught in a forest fire, bearing her high above the forest floor of the north woods. Swaying from branch to branch, just like he did in Africa.

"Northern Wisconsin." I shook my head. "Can you believe it? *Tarzan* in northern Wisconsin!"

She grinned, triumphant. "Told you." Then she propped her chin on her knees and stared out into the fog.

"That's where I'll be next month." Her voice was low, dreamy. "Camp Firefly is up north. Maybe the very same place. Or right next to it. There are lots of big trees."

I hadn't ever paid much attention to Heather's talk about summer camp. It was just some place she went every summer. But now all of a sudden "up north" sounded different. Exotic almost. If E.R.B. had picked it out of all the places on all the continents, it had to be the next best thing to Africa. For the first time I felt a little prick of jealousy. All the other E.R.B. things belonged to both of us: the boma, the cipher, the books.

"You're lucky. I've never been up north any more than I've been to Africa."

This time she shone her flashlight at me. Just before I blinked against the glare, I saw that look on her face, that cat-gleam I knew so well.

"Za—you come too!"

"To camp?"

"Yes, to camp. It's not too late to register."

"But—"

"Don't you see?" Her voice got louder, more excited. Her eyes practically glowed through the fog. "The book was a clue just now, telling us. Camp is *for* people like us. All those trees and lakes and wild animals and trails—it's the perfect idea!"

It was an impossible idea. Any other time I would have said so right away. I would have told her, "It would be nice, but I can't. The kids in my family don't go to camp." Camp and piano lessons and vacation trips went with families who had extra money left after the bills had been paid.

But this was the boma, the place for impossible things. And it was five twenty a.m. on a foggy morning when the whole world was wrapped in a dream cloud.

"It'd be so much more fun if you came, Za. Those other campers are just tarmangani. They don't know anything about real wild places, like we do."

"But I don't—"

"It's the next step, see? First one night out, in the boma. Then a whole week out, in the north woods. Same woods where *he* stayed." She tapped the book. "It's all part of our training in denizenship!"

Jungle fever was coming on. I could feel it in the prickly-itchy feeling on my arms, and the little voice in my head whispering, "Perfect! Think of it, Erin. Camp. And not just any camp. An E.R.B. camp."

I took a deep breath. "How much does it cost?"

"I don't know. Mom just pays it." She flicked her light on and off, thinking. "I think fifty . . . no, more like a hundred."

A hundred dollars. It might as well have been ten thousand. Heather looked at my face and changed her tone.

"Now I don't know for sure. I'm just guessing. It might not be so much. And you have *some* money, don't you?"

I had a jar on my closet shelf with some money. And I had a bank account that I started when I was in the second grade. It had about thirty-seven dollars in it last time I checked. And my birthday was only a few weeks away. Aunt Jeanne in Colorado usually sent money.

I bit my lip. Should I even be thinking about this, the way things were at home?

"You know, my dad doesn't always work," I said in a low voice. "So there's not too much money for things like camp."

She looked down. "I guess I shouldn't keep talking about camp. I'll shut up."

"*No.*" I said it much louder than I meant to. "No, really Mom likes us to have fun. And . . . it would be all right to ask for some, if I already had most of the money."

"It's just like this overnight, Za." She was eager again. "Staying here sounded impossible at first, too. But here we are. Think *yes* and it'll be *yes.* We'll make it happen."

She was right. Strange, but saying it would happen—maybe, made it feel like it could happen—maybe. Excitement prickled through my tired fuzzy head. I looked over the edge of the roof.

"Come on. Let's go down. Right now." What were we waiting for, anyway? Shivering and hiding up on the roof like coward tarmanganis. I jumped up and yanked down our tablecloth tent. Heather packed away the tools and books. Next we peeled off the clammy leopard skins.

"I've got a key. We can use the back door." With the leopard skin gone, she was just Heather again, practical, ordinary, down-to-earth Heather. "We'll have to be absolutely quiet. If they find out we're out this early . . . oh boy."

I started down the tree, climbing through ghost layers, feeling for the limbs I knew were there, waiting for me.

"Don't worry," I whispered. "We'll make it. And just think how fantastic that cocoa will taste!"

Nine

◙◙◙

The clock said eight o'clock when I walked into my living room with Heather's picture postcard of Camp Firefly tucked in my pocket and three cups of lukewarm lumpy cocoa sloshing around in my stomach.

Geri was talking on the phone and doing leg extensions at the same time, swinging her leg back and forth in the doorway.

"You eat a grapefruit with every meal," she said into the phone, "and you're supposed to lose five pounds the first week."

"Why don't you just have the receiver permanently attached to the side of your head?" I suggested on my way into the kitchen. She changed legs and turned around, ignoring me.

"That's right. Every meal, even dinner. Sue did it and it worked for her."

Grapefruit. Ugh. Probably start a chemical reaction with the cocoa in my stomach right now. What I needed was something filling. Something *sweet*. I started rummaging through the cupboards.

"Erin, don't eat the grapefruits. They're for my diet," Geri called, in her big sister voice, not her smile-into-the-receiver voice. "And Mom wants us to clean the house today, so stick around."

53

"We just cleaned it last weekend!" No way was I hauling around a vacuum cleaner right now. I barely had enough energy to haul my weary bones into my nice warm bed. "Mom didn't say anything to *me* about working on our very first day of vacation!"

Angry footsteps stomped into the kitchen. "Call you back later," she muttered into the phone. Then, facing me, "She told me, because *I'm* in charge. And you're *going* to help!"

"I'm *going* to eat. Then I'm *going* to my room." My eyes were gritty, my head was thick and fuzzy, and my clothes were still damp. My whole body longed to lie down. "I'll clean later."

"You are the most selfish, immature brat! You and Heather after school every day. You and Heather overnight, while I stay home with Katie and the work. You in your room every night. Are you part of this family or not, Erin Callahan?"

"I can't hear TV!" Katie yelled.

"Shut up." I aimed the words at both of them. And I pulled so hard on the bread drawer that it fell on the floor, right on my foot. "Now see what you made me do!"

I reached in to pull it back, and then I saw them, way back in the hollow place in the wall. Bottles. Two empty bottles. Green and glassy and evil. My stomach did a funny little turn. I looked up at Geri and aimed my thumb at the hole.

She pulled them out and heaved them into the trash bag so hard they broke in the sack. She glared after them, then at me. I glared back, grabbed the whole loaf of bread and took it with me down the hall, to my room. I was sorry I ever came home. The sacred mist of the boma was much better than this. I could eat my bread alone in my bedroom, or in the attic.

With one piece of bread dangling out of my mouth, and the loaf in my left hand, I reached up with my right to the closet shelf, for the money jar. I didn't have to reach as far back as usual. It stood at the very edge, almost falling off. And when I lifted it, it was much too light.

I knew even before I opened it and looked in. The money was gone.

"Quit hogging the bread." Geri poked her head in the doorway. Her voice was still angry. "We need it for—" And then the look on her face changed, when she saw my face.

"What happened?"

I shook the empty jar. No need to say anything. We looked at each other.

"How much was it?" Geri sat down on the bed.

I didn't answer. I stared at the bedspread hard, so she couldn't see the tears welling around my eyeballs.

"Erin—" Her fingers pulled at the bedspread fluff. "It's like . . . he's sick. Otherwise he wouldn't do things like . . . this."

The sickness was evil. He was an evil tarmangani. I blinked furiously.

"Anyway, he's gone. He won't be back for a while."

"How do you know?" My voice trembled.

She took a deep breath. "He's—he's in jail."

I looked up then. "What!" Did people get arrested for being too drunk? Did they *stay* in jail? "How come?"

"Mom doesn't want us to know. But I heard her talking on the phone. He was in a fight at Joe's. That's all I know." She got up, keeping her voice even, matter-of-fact. "*That's* why we're cleaning again. Airing the whole place out. See?"

Airing the place out. We always did that when he left. But we couldn't air out the shadow that stayed behind—in the backs of cupboards, and in my very own closet shelf.

I pulled out the postcard of Camp Firefly when Geri left. The lake and the woods stared back at me from far away.

No! I wasn't going to let it get unreal and far away. It was a real place. Heather had been there before. And I still had my bank book. And our plan. It was the next step, like Heather said. A place for denizens. It was meant to be.

I stuck the picture in the empty jar, so I could stare at it through the glass, like a framed picture. The excitement from the initiation was gone. Instead there was an angry stubborn feeling I'd never had before. I was *going* to camp.

Mom came in to my room after dinner. I knew right away that Geri had told her.

"How much was it?" she asked in a tight, clipped voice. "Two? Five? Ten? How much?"

I shrugged. After all, it wasn't her fault.

56

She opened her purse and took out a five dollar bill.

"That's all I can give you right now. Find a . . . safe place for your money from now on, Erin." Her face twisted a little, saying that.

I chewed my lip hard. My eyes went to the closet, to my trapdoor. There *was* a safe place. A safe and sacred place for my money and for me. I had to get back to Bal-Za—

Mom stood there a minute, watching me. "You're not going to stay here all evening, are you?" Her voice was a little warmer now, coaxing almost. "Sulking never helps anything, Erin. You know that."

"I'm not sulking." But of course she wouldn't understand. No one would. About Bal-Za.

Still she stayed in the doorway. Her eyes seemed to bore right through me. Then she glanced down the hall, where Geri's record player was working on the same old stack of singles, with her door shut, to drown out Katie's TV noise. Mom nodded to herself, like she'd just made a decision, then left.

I waited until her footsteps disappeared down the hall. Then I started gathering my things: my notebook, my money jar, my pen. I started toward the closet.

"Erin! Katie! Geri! I need your help. All of you."

Mom stood outside the kitchen door, with an old workshirt on, a ladder under her arm, and a determined look on her face.

"We're going to take down the storm windows

and get the screens up," she called out. "Let some fresh air into the house finally."

"Tonight?" Geri said incredulously. Mom was never energetic enough to start big projects after work. But here she was, smiling, waving us out the door.

"Get moving, before I remember how tired I am and change my mind. Hop to!" She pretended to crack a whip.

We hopped. Geri took down the storm windows, and I put up the screens, while Mom washed windows and Katie latched and unlatched hooks.

"Need any help with those?" Mr. Morris called out from his yard. He was wearing bib overalls and a funny-looking cap, and he had a big pair of pruning shears in his hands. It was hard to imagine him as a high school principal in that outfit.

"No thanks," Mom called back cheerfully. "The girls and I can get this one ourselves." She smiled at me as I staggered by with my oversized load. "Doesn't it feel good to be accomplishing something around here for a change?"

"Ugh," I grunted. Of course the screens needed to be put up. They should have been put up some time in May, even. But right now there were other things I'd rather be doing. Like Bal-Za—

Geri passed with her window.

"I am the viper," she whispered in a low, breathy voice. "I am ten blocks away."

She wanted me to say, "What's a viper?" I knew it. So I kept my lips firmly shut and tried to look very uninterested.

She came even closer on her next trip by.

"I am the viper. I am five blocks away," she hissed, drawing out each syllable in a low, ghostly voice.

I sighed. "All right, what's a viper?"

She gave me a smug grin and marched away with her window.

"Hey, Erin," she called a few minutes later, from the ladder.

"What?"

She changed her voice; rolled her eyes; held her arms out above her head. "I am the viper; I am *two* blocks away."

I giggled this time.

The next time we passed, she held up a bottle of Windex with a big dumb grin on her face.

"Hello. I am the viper, and I came to vipe your vindow."

I threw my dust rag at her. "Vipe your own vindow!"

Geri grinned proudly and wiped her hands on her jeans.

"Done with my story and done with the windows," she announced. "Time for my eight o'clock grapefruit." She checked her sideways reflection in the window, as she passed, sucking in her stomach.

"Some fat viper," I called out sweetly.

"Mommy, these hooks won't latch," Katie yelled out the window.

"Then we probably didn't get them matched up right." Mom turned to me. "Erin, would you get my basic tool kit?"

I caught Geri's eye. We both grinned. Mom's basic tool kit consisted of three things: crochet hook, crochet thread, and scissors.

A few minutes later, the window screen latches were all tied to their eyescrews with crocheted blue thread. Mom made triple knots.

"There, that ought to hold." She wiped her palms together with a satisfied nod.

"Mommy, that's the same kind of string that's on the refrigerator shelf that fell down, isn't it?" Katie asked.

"I did that one with a chain stitch to make it stronger. Everything in this house is held together with string and rubber bands, didn't you know that?"

Even Katie grinned.

Later, in my room, I tried to rekindle the Bal-Za feeling, to get back in the mood. But instead, I kept thinking of vipers and vindows and giggling. Besides, the cool breeze blowing through the newly opened window felt so good, I didn't really want to climb up to the hot attic.

Bal-Za's fate would have to wait a while longer.

Ten

□□□

Kudu shone hotter on the roof boma each day into summer. But the sweeping willow branches made a canopy of shade near the edge.

I swatted the gnat that landed on the cipher tablet. He made a little smear right across the two numbers that I had been staring at for ten minutes.

Eighty-five. Dollars.

"Mom said it went up since last year," Heather explained. "It was seventy-five."

It was a very long way from the thirty-seven dollars in my bank account.

I ran my fist down a small willow stem, ripping off leaves.

"Like I said in the beginning, I don't have enough money."

Heather cut in. "Like *I* said, we'll make enough. We'll make it our project, like the cipher and the overnight." She was using her stubborn, only-child voice. Heather was used to getting what she really wanted.

"I asked Mom this morning what would be a good way to earn money. She's always got ideas, like her refinishing and her rummage sales. You know what she said? 'Find your area of expertise and capitalize on it.' "

"Huh?"

Heather giggled. "That's what I said. So she told me that creative people find creative ways to make money. First you're supposed to find out what you're good at, then figure out a way to make money with it."

"Oh, I'd be just great with that stripper stuff and varnish."

"That's what she's expert at. Not us. We're experts at. . . ."

"Yes? Experts at what?" I challenged her.

"The . . . the jungle! That's what." She waved the cipher. "Jungle codes, jungle creatures, jungle lore. Right?"

"So what are we supposed to do, lead safaris? Charge admission to our boma?" I shuddered at the very idea. "Our jungle information is *private*."

Heather just kept staring down at the river.

"Jungle . . . jungle . . ." she murmured. "There should be *some* way."

The word hung there, a whisper under the wild willow branches. Jungle. There was something tantalizing about it. If we could do something that didn't give away any secrets—

"Too bad it's not Halloween," Heather said, chewing a strand of hair. "We could fix up our own spookhouse. Charge admission and . . ." She stopped. Her eyes got that glittery cat-gleam.

"*That's* what we can charge admission to! Not our boma."

"What?"

"A *jungle* house. How about it? We'll fix my garage up and maybe get a record of jungle noises; blindfold kids and have them walk through giant spider webs and hold naked eyeballs and things like that."

"Ye . . . ah, but will kids pay very much just to walk around blindfolded?" We'd need more than that. "And will your folks let us use your garage?"

"Sure. We'll go ask Mom now. Her rummage sale doesn't start for a while."

"No," Mrs. Prescott said right away, without even stopping to think about it for half a second. "Heather, for goodness sakes, you know I need the garage for the refinishing, like I'm doing right now." She looked grouchy and hot and tired.

"Darn those gnats!" She picked a tiny bug out of the just-varnished wood. "This chair is going to look like it has the measles." She sounded mad enough to swat at anything in her way. Heather gave the signal, and we started backing away.

"Heather. Erin." She set down her brush. "I'm sorry. I didn't mean to snap at you. And I don't want to wreck your plans. But using our garage is simply out of the question. If you're looking for something to do . . ." She paused, thinking, "There's the pool at the high school, and the tennis courts, and I think there's a workshop going on at the library. Puppets, that's it. I saw the poster about it yesterday."

"Sure, Mom. Great idea." Heather kept backing away. Then, under her breath, "Well, that's that. She thinks we're bored. Well, what about your place?"

"Puppets," I said slowly. "Heather, what about puppets? For the jungle house. A jungle puppet show! We could write the script and make the puppets, and put on the show in *my* garage." I could hear my voice getting louder, more excited, with each word. "Make the whole place look like a jungle!"

Heather grabbed my arm and pumped it up and down. "Erin, you're a genius! The little kids will come to watch the puppet show and the big kids will come for the scary parts. The blood and guts and spider webs. We could even serve refreshments. Jungle Potion!"

"And Bwarf. Don't forget the Bwarf."

She giggled and clapped me on the back. "For Bwarf they pay double. Camp Firefly here we come!"

Eleven

□□□

Our garage was about as dirty and neglected as an ancient jungle ruins. Since we didn't have a car anymore, we hardly ever opened the big door. When Heather and I finally got it to swing, a whole cloud of dust went up with it, making us cough and choke.

When the dust settled, we were staring at a year's supply of junk and grease and dirt.

"Wow." Heather's voice was low, impressed. She was used to her workshop garage. "I guess . . . we need . . . two brooms."

I gulped. "Well, it doesn't have to really end up clean, just cleared out some."

Our kitchen broom was so worn down it only counted as half a broom. But the Morrises had the big push kind.

"Cleaning the garage . . . well, good for you!" Mrs. Morris said when I asked to borrow it. "If you run out of things to sweep over there, just come on back."

I smiled at her, but I knew I'd need a dirt-detector before I'd find anything to sweep in the Morrises' spic-and-span yard.

"Here, take some cookies with you." She reached

into a pretty glass canister on the counter. "You'll need to keep your energy up."

"Thanks!" But I broke one apart on the way home and inspected it for green specks or other weird things. She even put *rhubarb* in cookies sometimes. These were okay, though. Just nuts and raisins.

We worked the whole afternoon, stacking greasy tools in a heap on the workbench, shoveling dirt into trash cans, and piling the clutter into a corner. It was hot, sweaty work.

There was something else wrong, too, besides the dirt and grease. Using my garage for the show had sounded like a good idea when we first talked about it. But now I wasn't so sure. Our garage *had* been used for something all this time. Dad would drink in here, when he didn't want anyone to know. It was his hideout, really. My eyes kept going to the door, half-expecting to see him there, with a long skinny liquor store bag in his hand.

He's *gone*, Erin. Keep sweeping. Time to clean out the garage, just like Mom did the house.

Heather wasn't nervous or worried. She didn't stop talking the whole afternoon.

"We have to let lots of people know about it," she said about twenty times. "That's how Mom gets people at her rummage sales. Advertising."

"How long is it going to take us to get ready?" I spoke loudly, trying to drown out that uneasy feeling.

Heather leaned on her broom. "Well, camp is

66

four weeks away. Fourth of July week. That's part of the fun, watching the fireworks over the lake."

"Then we'll set Jungle Day for two weeks away." I wanted to have extra time, in case we didn't raise enough from the show and from my birthday. In case I had to think of something else.

We tacked a piece of paper up on the wall and scribbled ideas as they popped into our heads. We even thought of a title for the project. A proper E.R.B. name. The Ara Project.

"Because Ara means lightning. And lightning bug is another name for firefly, as in camp," Heather said with a big grin. "You know, we're doing such a good job, your mom should *pay* us for cleaning up the place!"

"Fat chance." But then the smile froze on my face, as I opened one of the cupboard doors.

Bottles. Bottles. Bottles. Big green Gallo bottles, all heaped on top of each other, almost ready to fall out of the cupboard.

His lair, that's what it was. We'd invaded his lair. The tense nervous feeling washed over me, like a wave.

Well, what did I expect? I knew he came in here. And he doesn't drink the bottles, too. He had to find someplace to hide them.

I shut the cupboard door quickly and looked over at Heather. She was leaning on her broom, with a funny expression on her face. It was probably the first time in her life she'd ever seen so many empty liquor bottles crammed into one place.

"Does he come in here a lot, Erin?" Now she

was worried, too. "Maybe we should go someplace else—"

"No, it's okay." My voice was too loud. "He's gone now." Sometimes when he left, he stayed away for weeks, or even months. It would be like that this time, too. He wouldn't be back before Jungle Day. He *couldn't*.

Twelve

◧◫◩

"**I** cleaned the garage today," I announced at dinner. "With Heather."

No one was very impressed. Geri kept eating her spaghetti. Katie kept picking out the onions in her sauce. Mom was eating like a robot. Her mind was somewhere else. I cleared my throat.

"I cleaned it because we're going to have a puppet show in it." This time at least Katie looked up.

"Puppets? Can I do it, too?"

"You can watch. We're doing our show in two weeks," I said loudly. "It's a jungle story. We're going to charge admission."

Geri shook her head. "Those kinds of things never make much money," she said in her wise, older-sister voice. "Not magic shows or plays or Kool-Aid stands. Kids won't come if you charge much."

"Ours will. We're putting up posters to advertise. It's okay, isn't it, Mom? To use the garage?"

"What?" She came back from her faraway thinking place and looked at me, finally. "A jungle play? The garage? Yes, I suppose. But there's something else we need to talk about tonight." She set down her fork and took a deep breath.

69

"I talked to a realtor today. He's coming by to-night to see the house. I think we may be putting it up for sale." She said it as matter-of-factly as if she was saying, "I think we may be vacuuming."

I let a whole bundle of spaghetti slip off my fork.

"What!"

Mom set down her coffee cup. "You know, girls, I'm tired of the cleaning that goes with a big house. And there are a lot of repairs needed that I can't begin to take care of. It's really more house than we need right now. Anyway, when you're renting and something breaks, you just call up the landlord and tell him to fix it." Her voice was light, happy even. I looked at her suspiciously. Sometimes it was hard to tell when Mom was putting on an act.

"Will the new house have a swing set?" Katie asked. "Can I bring all my toys?"

I looked around the kitchen and out into the hall. It wasn't too much house. It was just the right amount of house. It had my room, my attic, my garage.

Garage! "We won't move before Jungle Day, will we?" I asked, feeling suddenly breathless. "It's in two weeks."

"No, Erin," Mom said with a small brittle laugh. "Not before your Jungle Day. So you don't have to worry."

But I did. I had a lot to worry about. Camp, money, a million details of the Ara Project and now —losing my house.

But I kept my thoughts to myself until later, when Geri and I were doing dishes.

"But I don't see why we have to move all of a sudden!" I rubbed the towel on the plate so hard it squeaked. "It doesn't matter that we can't fix everything. And Mom doesn't even do the housecleaning. We do."

"It's because of *money*," Geri hissed. "And it didn't happen all at once. It's been happening for a long time. Dad owes a lot of money. And we have to sell the house to pay the debts."

Dad again. Everywhere we turned. We could throw away bottles and open windows, but the shadow was so big, it was going to gobble up our whole house now.

After dark I climbed up to the attic. I had been so busy thinking about camp and the Ara Project, I still hadn't gotten Bal-Za out of Azumba.

She was ready now. She had planned every detail carefully. She knew when her captors slept. She knew where the keys were kept. She knew the layout of the city; which parts of the stone wall surrounding the city were guarded, and which part had a small crumbling hole—small enough for a slim body to slip through. . . .

And be swallowed by the waiting jungle.

Thirteen

◻◻◻

"**B**ad. Terrible!" I tore up my third try at a puppet script and threw it in the wastebasket. "I can't give away any of the stories about Tarzan and Korak; they're our secret. But I can't think of anything else!"

Heather looked up from the floor, where she was coloring a poster. "Why don't you look through the E.R.B. box? I think there's other ones besides Tarzan, down at the bottom."

Dust and grit covered my fingers, as I dug down through the half-rotted bindings toward the bottom. They were in worse shape than the Tarzan books.

"There's some about Mars and some about Venus, and—here's one about some place I never heard of. Pellucidar." I picked it up and thumbed through the thick yellow pages.

"Hey!" I waved it in front of Heather. "This is it! Perfect! It's about a world *inside* the earth. A big prehistoric jungle full of dinosaurs. And the sun is right smack in the middle. It just hangs there. So it's always daytime, and there aren't any seasons. Isn't that fantastic!" I paged through, looking for pictures.

Heather's eyes gleamed. She held up her poster.

"Can't you just see it in big letters: 'PELLUCIDAR: WORLD INSIDE THE EARTH!' Erin, it sounds great!"

I worked on the script that night. An explorer and his son find Pellucidar while they're exploring an extinct volcano. In the jungles of Pellucidar all sorts of things happen to them. My pen could hardly keep up with them. The boy, Philip, gets lost, then almost killed by a dinosaur, then saved in the nick of time by a native girl. I called her Pella. She shows him the wonders of her world, then he and his father finally return to their own land, with fond good-byes.

"Great!" Heather cried, when I read it to her. "It's got everything: dinosaurs, jungles, danger, suspense, even romance, almost. We're in business! Tomorrow we find a box for the theater, then start on the puppets, right?"

We shook on it. We were organized, creative, capable businesswomen, just like Heather's mom. Things were falling right into place.

Until that night, at dinner.

"There will be some people looking at the house over the weekend," Mom said. "So I'd like you girls to do some real cleaning for me these next few days. We've just been dusting off the top layer for a long time. We're going to have to get at some of the real grime, make the house look as good as we can. It'll be a job, but it's important."

I stared at her. Spend the whole day scrubbing when—I couldn't!

"Mom," I tried to sound as agreeable as possible, "you see, tomorrow Heather and I. . . ."

"Erin." Her voice was flat, definite. "I know you're working on your big show. But this has *got* to be done, and Geri is *not* going to do it all. Do you understand ?"

"But—"

"*Do you understand?*"

There was no arguing with that voice.

"Yes." My voice was sullen.

Her eyes held mine; I couldn't look down. In that long second, it felt like she was looking right through me.

"We all have to pitch in and help around here, Erin. And don't you forget it."

"Mom doesn't ask you to help very often, you know," Geri said later, over dishes. "Do you have to make such a big stink, just because she wants the house to look decent for a change?"

"We can't change the date for our Jungle Day. We can't advertise a puppet show and then not have it!" But no one around here cared about that.

"Puppets." Geri shook her head. "Puppets!"

Puppets. I thought about them the whole morning, while I scrubbed the bathroom. Geri gave me the worst job out of spite. I knew it. I hate scrubbing toilets. I hate getting long hair out of sinks. I hate scouring bathtub rings that have been ignored for months.

The phone rang three times. Geri's friends. Karen, Mona, Sue. I'd never really met any of them, just their voices. They might as well have been ghosts that haunted telephone receivers: "Is Geri there?" "Can I talk to Geri?"

"I thought we were supposed to be working!" I yelled around the corner, on the last ring.

"Long cord!" Geri called back with a grin. She was holding the receiver between her shoulder and ear and dusting. "I swept with Karen, did the kitchen with Mona, and now I'm dusting with Sue."

Someone knocked at the door. The most welcome sound all day. *My* friend. With a big bag of jungle decorations.

I gave the floor a last wipe and emptied the rest of the cleanser down the toilet in a big blue foamy flush.

"Done with the bathroom," I yelled. "And I can't do anything else. There's no more cleanser!"

"Wait!" Geri yelled. "There's—"

But I didn't stick around to hear what other tortures she had in store for me. I ran out the back door and into the garage with Heather.

"Good old Mom and her rummage sale junk." Heather held up a big wad of plastic leaves and vines and flowers. "She gave these to me. I think she's trying to be extra nice, because she didn't let us use the garage. She's even letting me use one of her good green sheets, with the leaves all over it."

We tacked the sheet over the back wall, and we hung the strands of green flowers over the side wall. The effect wasn't too jungly. Putting one of the posters up helped. So did small branches from the backyard tree. We were trying to figure out where to get some trailing vines when Geri marched in. She was holding Katie by the hand.

"All right," Geri said, barely giving a glance to our artistic effects. "If you're going to sneak out after just one teeny room and that only half-clean, then you can do your share by watching Katie, now and the rest of the week." She turned to Katie.

"Erin and Heather are going to make puppets, Katie," she said in a completely different voice, all icky-sweet. "Won't that be fun? You can help." And she stomped back into the house, leaving us with our plastic vines, our green sheet, and Katie.

Fourteen

□□□

At first Katie just wheeled the shopping cart around the driveway, while we hung decorations inside. She was proud of the shopping cart. We were probably the only people on the block with a real grocery store cart parked in the driveway, instead of a car. But it was the best way to get lots of bags of groceries home, and we always brought each one back on the next big trip. So far, no one had ever tried to stop us.

"Here, Katie, you play grocery store," I said sweetly, feeling very smug and smart, as I ducked back into the garage.

My plan worked. For two and a half minutes.

"Erin! Erin!" She was scrunched into a ball in the cart, with her hands covering her head, and screaming. "A bee! He's gonna sting me. A bee!"

"Careful, dummy, you'll knock the whole cart over." I yanked her out. "Look, it's just a sweat bee."

"He's gonna sting me!" Her arms went around my neck like a vise.

"Let go; you're strangling me! What a sissy." All white-faced and shaky at a little old sweat bee.

"Some denizen she'd make." Heather poked me.

She started jumping around, yelling, "Help, Erin, it's Numa; he's gonna get me. Help!"

I pried Katie's arms loose from around my neck and put her down. "Look, if you're so scared out here, Katie, come in the garage with us. Just don't *touch* anything, you hear?"

Heather and I had done a good job sweeping up the garage. But of course, we didn't get every single spider out. And of course, Katie found the one we missed. A big hairy one with a huge web around him up in the corner.

"Erin! There's a tarantula!" She ran back out to the yard, tripped on our pile of jungle branches, and started howling.

"What a *crybaby!*" It was embarrassing for a true denizen to be related to such a tarmangani sissy. And pest besides.

"We'll never get anything done with her around," Heather hissed under her breath.

I marched in the house.

Geri was lying in her bedroom, staring at the ceiling.

"Oh, you're really working hard," I said.

"I cleaned the kitchen. I vacuumed. I dusted. And now I'm releasing my inhibitions." She spoke in her very calm dramatic voice.

"Well I'm *done* watching Katie. She's ruining my whole afternoon. I'm not going to do it any more!"

"Oh yes you are. All week. I haven't even started on the basement yet."

I felt like a volcano ready to boil over. But I

didn't even get a chance to complain to Mom. She was tired and hassled when she got home from work.

"Some people are coming to see the house tonight," she said at dinner. "We have to finish eating early." Her voice sounded on edge. She leaned back in her chair and wiped her hand across her forehead. "It's hot."

Dessert was strawberries from the Morrises' garden. Geri had splurged and got spray whipped cream. But by dessert time, Mom was really in a hurry.

"No time to chat over dessert," she said. "Finish and take your plates out."

Geri aimed the squirter at the strawberries and pushed the nozzle. A big fizzle noise came out, but no whipped cream.

"Here, give it to me. You don't do it like that!" Mom snapped, grabbing the can. She aimed it down. But she hadn't checked where the nozzle was. A big foamy mess whooshed across the table and plopped on the wall.

"Damn." Mom turned the can, but her finger was still part way on the nozzle. Whipped cream still oozed out, all over her blouse and arm.

We all stared. She stood there with a big scowl. I waited for the next cuss word. Then Geri reached over and grabbed the can.

"Here, give it to me. You don't do it like that!" she snapped, in perfect imitation of Mom's voice.

Mom looked at her a minute. Then she put her hand up to her mouth. The sound that came out next sounded a lot like a giggle.

I giggled too. So did Geri. And Katie. It was really very funny all of a sudden. The wall, the white puddles on the table, Mom's cream-covered arm. I hiccupped into my strawberries.

The can really did work. Geri smothered the strawberries with big creamy lumps, while Mom wiped her eyes with her napkin.

"I hope I never get so old that I lose my sense of humor," she gasped, between giggles. And it didn't even matter that the realtors picked that minute to knock on our door.

Fifteen

◻◻◻

"Well, that's that," I said to Heather. "We're stuck with her. All week. Mom took Geri's side."

We both stared at Katie. She looked innocent enough, standing right outside the door. But she hadn't found anything with antennae or stingers or hairy legs yet.

"Mom just kept saying, 'Find something for her to do. Then she won't bother you.'" I sighed, a big martyr's sigh. "Well, may as well try it."

"Here, Katie," I called out in my best big sister voice. "The cupboard over here needs dusting. Would you do it?" I tossed her the rag, then scooted up on the sawhorse next to Heather. "That ought to keep her busy for a while." I started shaping my papier-mâché into a puppet head, like we learned in art. There was so much to do! First the heads, then costumes, props, more decorations, the theater—

"Erin, let me do a puppet."

"We'll let you do one later." That was a lie, but sometimes you have to lie to little kids to shut them up. Katie would make a gooey mess out of the mâché, and we needed all of it, anyway.

81

She threw down her rag. "I'll make my own puppet."

"Come right back," I yelled, as she ran toward the house. Then I bent over my puppet head, pressing, shaping. The face took a lot of concentration. I didn't even notice how much time had passed, until I saw Katie's rag on the floor and remembered that she hadn't come back yet.

"I'd better go see where Katie is." I said it calmly, but I ran into the house. If she got into something she shouldn't—

I opened the kitchen door and stared.

Katie was kneeling on a kitchen chair. On the table were about ten or twelve eggs, scissors, magic markers, glue, pipe cleaners, buttons. The eggs must have been the hard-boiled ones, because she had done *everything* to them, and there wasn't a sign of raw yolk.

One egg had two moving eyes glued on and construction paper feet. He was colored yellow. The one beside him had moving eyes too, and a beak. He had so many shell cracks, he was practically peeled. And beside him was a black one with three bent pipe cleaner legs on each side. An ugly, black, just-hatched, spidery thing.

"I'm making puppets," Katie said matter-of-factly. "Doo-del puppets."

I stared at her. What would Mom think of all these inked-up, ruined eggs and the mess all over the table? And how had Katie managed to get to kindergarten without knowing that a puppet is something you put your hand in?

Any other kid would have used socks or paper bags. Not Egg-Head Katie.

"Easter's over," Heather said behind me. She had a wicked grin on her face. I just groaned. All this mess to clean up, and our mâché pulp getting hard in the garage.

Katie picked up the spider egg and held it out proudly.

"It's my spider doo-del," she said in her low voice. "I'm not scared of these kind."

"If you kept it in the refrigerator," Heather said slowly, "we could hang it, for jungle scenery. It does look like a big spider."

"But these are her *dinner*," I said. "That's all she eats is eggs. We can't hang her dinner all over the garage! And if it fell--" I giggled, "it'd be a Humpty Dumpty spider!"

Heather started giggling, too. "Hey, Katie, how come they're doo-dels?"

Katie pulled a magazine from the chair beside her. "They're here," she said, holding up the page. "All the doo-dels."

Sure enough, little egg-shaped creatures covered the page. And sure enough the title said: "Make Your Own Scary Doodle-Bug Creatures." I stared down at Katie again. Could the little brat *read*?

"Hey!" Heather grabbed the magazine. "Would you look at that? Those are jungle bugs, Erin!" Her eyes skimmed the page. "It says you can make them with dough or clay or—mâché!"

Our eyes met over Katie's head. "Do you think. . . ."

"Get down, Katie." I pulled her out of her chair. "We'll clean up the mess and put these in the refrigerator, and you can make more doo-dels out in the garage. OK?"

By the end of the afternoon our puppet heads were done and drying beside ten strange creatures with wadded up, papier-mâché bodies and pipe cleaner legs. And in the refrigerator lay the world's first hard-boiled spider.

Sixteen

ⵁ⵿ⵁ

Five days until Jungle Day. The puppets were all painted and costumed. The cave girl, Pella, had a leopard skin tunic. The boy, Philip, had a denim outfit that looked too much like a jean skirt. Tyrannosaurus was shaped more like an oversized alligator than a dinosaur, but he had nice fierce-looking teeth.

Heather turned the Dad explorer puppet over in her hand. She frowned. "He needs something. I know, what about a hat? The kind that look like hard hats. I think I saw an explorer on TV with that kind, once."

"A hard hat?" I looked at her. There was a hard hat on the shelf in Mom and Dad's closet. It was from a job that Dad had a long time ago. He used to let me wear it once in a while when I was little.

"I think I can get one. A big one, I mean," I said slowly. "We could use it for a model."

"Yeah, go get it."

"I'll be right back." I ran across the yard and into the house. But halfway down the hall, my steps slowed. And even though I couldn't hear Geri anywhere close, I stopped for a second at the door to Mom's room.

85

It wasn't wrong to go in there. Mom loaned me stuff all the time. And Dad probably didn't even remember he owned the hat. It would just take a second to run in and get it.

Still, I felt uneasy. I never went in there. When Dad was home, when he was drinking, it was always so smelly and messy. And when he wasn't home, well, it was *Mom's* room.

The timid, nervous feeling made me mad. I took a deep breath and hurried over to the closet.

Dresses, skirts, blouses, slacks on one side; the other side had a few old suits and lots of empty hangers. He'd taken most of his clothes with him. But he wouldn't have needed the hard hat. I pulled a chair over and stood on it, to check the shelf.

Sweaters and long underwear of Mom's, old baby books, a fishing cap, blankets, and in the far back corner—the hard hat.

I lifted it slowly, being careful not to knock anything else. But there was an old photo album wedged behind the hat. I just barely grabbed it in time, before it toppled off the shelf.

The album was so old some of the pages started to fall out when I tried to lift it back up. The pictures were all old-fashioned looking.

I'd never seen the pictures or the album before. I sat down on the chair and opened it up.

The pictures were of Mom and Dad a long time ago. Dad was thinner. His hair was wrong. Too slicked down. In the top picture he had his arm around . . . Mom?

I stared at the lady in the picture. She was young

and pretty, with a happy smile across her face, and an old-fashioned flowery dress. Was that really Mom?

Maybe it was the hair style. I tried covering the hair in the picture with my fingers. Strange, the face staring up at me looked an awful lot like Geri.

I turned the page. More old pictures. And, wonder of wonders, there was Dad in work clothes, wearing his hard hat! Was that one of his first jobs? Or some important promotion? Was that why he had his picture taken in it, and kept the hat all these years?

"Erin!"

I jumped in my chair.

"What are you doing, snooping around in Mom's closet! And what have you got? You're not supposed to be in here!"

I held up the album. "Did you ever see these pictures?" Geri loved looking through old baby books and pictures.

"Where did you get it?" Her voice was loud, accusing.

"The closet. I was just borrowing Dad's old hat. This was way in the back. Look." I flipped back to the first picture. "Mom looked like you, Geri, only with a different hair style." I used my friendliest tone, trying to get her curious, so she'd snoop too.

"Wow, was she ever skinny! And did she ever wear her hair long! And look at the way she used to pluck her eyebrows." My plan worked. Geri had the book in her lap now, with her face about six inches from the pictures.

"I think they were just married, in this picture. They used to go dancing a lot. Mom loves to dance.

And Dad's a great dancer." Geri's voice was dreamy. "I mean, he *used* to be. He even used to dance with me, when I was Katie's age." And then her voice changed to a mutter. "Katie'd sure never want to dance with him. She doesn't even know him. Not the way he was."

She looked up at me. "Erin, do you remember any of it . . . before?"

I nodded. Something inside me tensed. We never talked about "before."

She touched the hard hat. "Dad was an inspector, you know. He'd go around to all these different companies—"

"Really?" Dad, in charge of things, telling other people what to do, instead of washing dishes in a restaurant kitchen? But then, when I thought more about it, it didn't really seem so unbelievable. Dad loved bossing everyone around, when he was okay.

"And he made lots of things on his workbench in the garage. He made the toybox."

We looked at each other.

"The one he burned?"

"Yeah."

Geri shut the album and got up. "Better put it back, exactly where it was," she said, her voice blank.

I nodded. I knew now why Mom had shoved it far back in the closet corner. It hurt, remembering. But it was so rare to be talking about it like this. I didn't want to stop, even though the words came slow and fumbling.

"When did he start . . . drinking?"

"Around the time Katie was born. Mom was

really sick when she was pregnant with Katie. She had to stay flat on her back a long time."

"So?" I looked at her, confused. "What does that have to do with it?"

"There was a lot for Dad to do all of a sudden." Geri shook her head. "Mom says he just couldn't handle it—plus he was worried about her. He'd always had a few drinks when he came home from work late at night. But then he started drinking during the day. Like when he drove to these different companies, he'd stop off at bars first." Her tone went flat. "So—he lost his job. Then it got really bad."

She stared at me. "Don't you remember all this?"

I shrugged. I did and I didn't. Mostly the memories all ran together in my head—the comings and goings, the fights, the good and bad times. I couldn't sort it out.

But for Katie, it was all bad memories. Katie didn't really know Dad at all. She probably didn't even know he made the toybox, just that he burned it. If she tried to think back, what would she remember? The day Dad took her and me to a bar downtown, and we sat on a big stool in the darkened room, drinking Kiddie Cocktails with cherries?

Katie had missed all of the good times "before." I was suddenly glad we had let her make her doo-dels for Jungle Day.

I looked from the hard hat in my hands to the cigarette burn marks in the dresser top. I didn't understand. I never would.

Seventeen

◻◻◻

"What did you do, take a nap in there?" Heather called through the back door. "You were gone so long, I had time to make a new jacket for Philip. How do you like it?"

"Great," I said. But my mind was still on the conversation back in the bedroom.

"You know," Geri said slowly, "these kinds of shows don't really make you very rich. Lots of kids don't want to pay."

"We're already making money," Heather shot back. "Mom and Dad both paid seventy-five cents, even though they can't come. So did my grandma. The money's rolling in."

"Mrs. Morris gave me some money, too," I added. "Katie told her all about our show over the fence yesterday."

"So what are you going to do with all your fabulous riches then?" Geri said with a smug, big-sister smile.

"None of your business," I shot back, sending a secret, sideways glance at Heather.

Geri shrugged. "I've got better things to think about, anyway. Mona's coming by in a few minutes. There's a sale on at the mall."

90

I looked up suspiciously. "Does that mean—"

"Yes. You can stick around for once. This will be the very first and the only time I've gone shopping all summer." She was bossy big sister again. The close sharing moment was gone.

"Sure." I straightened. "*I* do all the work while *you* go have fun."

"Oh, that's really the way it is around here, all right," she said scornfully.

"That's the way it's getting to be, all right!"

In answer, she turned on a big phony smile. "There's chicken in a casserole dish in the fridge. Just stick it in the oven at three fifty for an hour and a half. And throw the last two loads in Matilda."

A car honked outside.

"*Byee*," Geri called on her way out the door.

"*She's* got better things to do!" I slammed the door after her. "*She's* got better things to think about! What does she think *we're* doing, twiddling our thumbs?"

So, while the theater and props waited out in the garage, and Heather started home, I threw the chicken in the oven, set the timer, turned on the TV for Katie, and tried to balance the clothes and the detergent just right, so Matilda would cooperate. I even patted her on the lid. "You can do it, Matilda, old girl," I told her, just like Geri and Mom.

Matilda was agitating full speed ahead on her load, jiggling across the floor, when Mom walked in.

"You cooking dinner, Erin?" She looked surprised.

"Chicken," I said casually. I didn't mention

91

that Geri made it, just kept bustling around the kitchen, setting the table, looking very efficient and organized.

Then it happened—right about the same minute that Geri walked in the door.

Wheeze. Whine. Matilda was trembling much too hard. Spatter. Wheeze. KLANG. Then—silence.

Geri stopped in her tracks. "What did you do to Matilda?" she whispered, horrified.

"I didn't do anything to Matilda!"

Mom strode across the kitchen, toward the very quiet washing machine. She opened the lid. I peeked in with her. The clothes were still there. And the water. Just sitting there.

Mom pushed the start knob in and out, gave a whack on one side, then the other.

"Maybe she just jiggled herself unplugged," I said hopefully. I tried to look behind the machine. All I could see were cobwebs.

"Let's move her."

With all of us grunting and shoving, we managed to push Matilda out a few inches, enough to see lots more cobwebs and dust clumps.

Mom peered back. She wrinkled her nose at the dust.

"It's not the plug. Maybe the belt broke."

"Do you want your basic tool kit, Mom?" Katie asked hopefully.

Mom shook her head, with a little grin. "I don't think my tool kit would do much good this time, Katie. I think old Matilda has waltzed her last waltz. She's given up the ghost."

"Aren't belts fixable?"

"Not at this stage of the game. She's too old to be putting money into her—if we had it, which we don't."

"Was it—my fault? Did I put the clothes in wrong?" My voice sounded small, squeaky almost.

Mom put her arm around my shoulder. "Of course not! The old girl's been living on borrowed time for quite a while. If this hadn't happened tonight, it would have tomorrow, or the next time we washed."

Geri took the vase of marigolds off the kitchen table and set them on the lid of the washing machine. She put her hand over her heart.

"Here lies Matilda," she intoned in a solemn voice. "She led a long and useful and *clean* life. She had a very *bubbly* personality." A giggle slipped out, wrecking her solemn expression. "We will remember her always."

I put my hand over my heart, too. "Amen."

Right on cue, the stove buzzer sounded.

"My chicken," I cried. But Geri reached the kitchen first. She came back a few seconds later, holding the casserole dish, without any potholders.

"Uh, Erin," she said sweetly, "just think how much better it would have cooked if you'd turned the oven on." She held the dish under my nose. Raw chicken stared up at me.

"Now what are we gonna eat?" Katie whimpered.

"Oh good Lord," Mom sat down in the kitchen chair. "If it's not one thing, it's another."

It was silly, but tears were starting behind my eyeballs. Here I'd given up my whole afternoon practically, and nothing was going right!

"I don't like that kind of chicken." A big tear rolled down Katie's face.

"Erin, you klutz! The one time I leave you to do dinner and—"

"That's enough," Mom said firmly. "Put the chicken in the refrigerator. We can cook it tomorrow."

"But what about. . . ?"

Mom reached for her purse and dumped the change from the coin purse onto the table.

"Fifty, seventy-five, a dollar, a dollar-fifty, two dollars, two-fifty," she mumbled, counting quarters. Then she opened the bill section. Here's a five. That makes seven-fifty. . . ."

"You need more? I have some change left from the scarf I bought at the mall." Geri started rummaging through her purse, too. She dumped three quarters on the table.

"That'll do it." Mom scooped it all back in her purse and snapped it shut decisively. She stood up. "It's certainly not enough for a new washing machine, but—" and a smile stretched across her face, "it *is* enough for hamburgers and fries."

My eyes opened wide. I saw Geri's and Katie's mouths hang open, as we all listened to the next words. Rare words around our house.

"In honor of this solemn occasion of no washing machine and no chicken—girls, we're dining out tonight."

Eighteen

◻◻◻

It was hard to get to sleep that night. My stomach was too full from the hamburgers, and my head was too full of thoughts from the day. Thoughts about the album, the puppet show, the dinner fiasco. And the feeling that we were running out of time for Jungle Day.

The thoughts turned into dreams.

I was sitting beside Heather in a car; we were riding through a beautiful woodsy place with huge trees on either side. We drove under a big banner that read "Camp Firefly." We got out of the car and ran toward the jungle lake. I was so happy. I flung my arms out and yelled: "I'm here! I'm here! I'm Erin, Lord of the Jungle!"

But then a big scaly creature rose up from the water and started padding toward us up the banks. Was it Gimla, the crocodile? No, it was bigger than that. And growing, getting larger. . . .

A dinosaur! Tyrannosaurus! He was coming right toward us. Suddenly Heather was gone. I was alone, running from the huge monster. And the landscape was getting more wild. Not birch and pine anymore, but huge tropical plants, growing so thickly that I had to fight my way through the undergrowth.

I could feel the eyes of other creatures, watching. Sheeta, Histah, Numa—

It wasn't camp at all. It was jungle Africa! I thrashed through the vines, running faster, trying to get away.

My hair caught on a vine. When I tried to pull free, I saw that it was the wrong color. Long and blond, instead of short and brown. I looked down at my clothes, my skin. They were wrong, too.

I wasn't me, at all. I was Bal-Za. Bal-Za, escaped from Azumba, yet still trapped by the teeming jungle. I had to get away, had to search for my father.

There was someone moving high above the jungle floor, grasping jungle vines, hurtling through the air. Now he was dropping to the ground, running toward me.

He was still too far away to see clearly, but something deep inside me knew that stride, that figure. My heart started pounding. I began to run, too—

Then I stopped. Up close, he looked different. Older, shorter. And his face was changing, flickering into another familiar face. I took a step back. He was wearing a hard hat. And there was a cigarette in his hands.

"No!" I tried to yell, but my voice stuck in my throat. "He's the wrong one! That's Erin's dad. I'm Bal-Za. It's wrong!"

He came toward me, smiling. "I'm the inspector around here," he called out in a loud, important voice.

I took another step back. The jungle was receding. But he was still walking toward me, still calling, shouting—

My eyes opened. The jungle vanished, but the shouting didn't. It was coming from the living room. I rubbed my eyes hard, trying to rub away the grogginess. Then my whole body froze, as the voices got louder.

Mom's. And . . . Dad's. I could only catch pieces of sentences.

"So help me, I'm not going to put up with it again. I'm warning you."

Then Dad's voice. Lower, deeper. I couldn't catch the words. I put the pillow over my head and squeezed my eyes shut. I was still shaky from the nightmare. Bal-Za, me. Camp Firefly, Africa. Dad, Tarzan. All mixed-up horribly. All wrong. And now Dad's voice in the other room. Maybe when I woke up again in the morning, it would be just another dream.

It wasn't a dream. I could see him sitting at the kitchen table across from Mom, as I walked down the hall for breakfast.

"No, no, no," yelled the voice inside my head. "He can't be back now. There are only two days left until Jungle Day."

I kept walking slowly, my hand trailing the wall, my eyes taking in everything: his clothes, neat and clean, his hair all combed, and his face shaved. He looked handsome, even jaunty sitting there at the table, blowing smoke toward the salt shaker.

97

He was back for another try, then. He'd probably be out job hunting most of the day. Maybe he'd find a job right away. Then he'd stay away from the garage and our jungle props.

It wasn't very reassuring. Sometimes his new tries only lasted a few days. I thought of all those green bottles locked up in the garage. He'd come out there a lot, before.

Mom set down her coffee cup and faced him. "I'm leaving for work now. Remember—" There was a warning note in her low voice.

"*I know.*" Dad stood up, too. He put his arm around her and kissed her.

I stood in the shadows of the hall, watching. A funny feeling washed through me, seeing Mom lean back for just a moment on Dad's shoulder, seeing them close, romantic almost. Like she really did . . . love him, maybe. Could she still love him?

Don't be stupid, I told myself. They're married, after all. They're your parents.

"Hey, there's my girl!" Dad smiled a big friendly smile as I walked into the kitchen. Time for my hug. He smelled good. But my stiff body wouldn't relax.

"Well, Erin Go Bragh." He sat down and leaned the chair back on two legs, cupping the lighter in his hands. His eyes teased me above the lighter. "If I'm not mistaken, you have a birthday coming up before too long. Number twelve, right?" He nodded, a slow thoughtful nod. "We'll get you a pretty dress; get you out of those jeans for once."

I stared down at the flecks of gold in the Formica tabletop and scraped my toes on the floor. When I

98

was younger, I really believed him, when he promised gifts or money. But things changed so fast. *He* changed so fast. You just couldn't count on it.

His blue eyes watched me, watched my reaction. The smile left his face. He leaned forward suddenly, putting the chair back on all four legs.

"Erin, listen to me. I'll tell you now, and I'll tell your sisters later when they get up. Things are going to be different around here. Believe me." His voice was very low and firm. "I'm going for a job interview this morning. I'll be working again."

I squirmed on my chair. "Uh, good," I said, staring even harder at the table flecks.

"Don't believe it," hissed the little warning voice. "You know you can't count on that, either. He means it now, but he won't later."

But he sounded so earnest. Like he *did* really mean it. It was so confusing, the tug-of-war feeling inside me. Wanting him here, liking him so handsome and confident, caring about me and my birthday. And wanting him to leave, before all the bad things started up again. I didn't understand it, any of it.

I was very glad to hear Heather's knock at the door, and see her face peering in through the screen. Nice cheery dependable Sabora.

"Heather's here now. We'll be—out there." I pointed at the garage, and my heart did a little two-step, thinking about that cupboard and Dad. I almost ran to the door. "Bye."

Heather was in a great mood.

"Erin, I had the best idea last night. We can tie

99

a rope to the rafters and charge the little kids for jungle swing rides! Ten cents a swing." She pulled a rope out of her backpack. "Mom gave me this. All we have to do is figure out how to tie it up and put a big knot at the bottom for sitting."

It was easier said than done. Even with the ladder, we couldn't get the rope tied to the rafter right. And it hung too far down, and the scissors couldn't cut through.

"It has to be a really good knot. We could get *sued* if someone fell on the cement."

"What the—" Dad stood leaning against the doorjamb, his hands in his pockets, staring at us.

"It's our jungle decorations," I said quickly. I tried to sound very firm and businesslike. "We've been working *weeks* to get it all up. We'll be here all day today. And tomorrow." Then, because I sounded so cold, I added, "Do you like it?"

"Looks . . . real nice. A jungle, huh?" He sounded friendly enough, but my muscles tightened, watching him. Did he wish we weren't here? Did he want the garage back the way it was?

Heather felt uncomfortable around him, I could tell. She was suddenly very busy with the rope, trying to force the scissors through.

"Not like that." Dad went over to his toolbox and pulled out a jackknife. "This'll cut your rope." He tossed it to me. "Keep it," he said with a wink. "Every jungle girl should have one. I've got others."

"Thanks!" A big wave of relief flooded through me. He was helping. He didn't mind that we were using his garage. And he'd told me just this morning

—things were going to be different around here. I knew better than to really count on promises, but ... you never knew. It could happen.

He squinted up at the mass of coils and loops we'd made to hold our rope to the rafter. "I think you need some help with that knot, too." His hands worked fast and sure, changing our wad into a sturdy compact knot. He grinned at us, climbing off the ladder. "That better?"

"Perfect." I gave it a trial swing. "Your knot's a lot better than ours!"

"It just takes practice. Same as this." He winked again, while his hands moved in fast, easy rhythm. Snap, snap, clap. Snap, snap, clap.

I glanced at Heather. She was watching carefully.

"Hey, that's good." She sounded surprised.

I grinned at her and lifted my hands. I couldn't resist it. Snap, snap, clap. Snap, snap, clap. I didn't know if I could keep up with Dad or not. But with Heather standing there all bug-eyed, I had to try.

Dad's fingers moved faster, challenging me. I tried to keep up, stubbornly.

Snap-snap-clap-snap-snap-clap-snap-snap-clap. My knuckles were going to cave in; my fingertips were numb; my palm was sore; my fist muscles were sagging. My snap turned into a clap, and I gave up, and we were all laughing.

I shook my hands out. "I think my fingers are going to fall off!"

"How did you learn that?" Heather demanded.

I nodded toward Dad. "He taught me." I felt a

quick stab of pride, saying that. He looked strong in that denim shirt with the sleeves rolled up. He was good at lots of things. Heather didn't know that. Lots of people didn't.

Still, I watched nervously, as he looked around the garage some more. Was he staring longer at the cupboards that I'd tied shut with cord and covered with plastic vines? My stomach tightened again. Or was it just my imagination?

"We're putting on a puppet show. We'll be practicing all day today and tomorrow." He had to know that the garage was *mine* right now. "Do you want to come?"

"Umm," he said, still glancing around the room. "We'll see. Well, good luck, jungle girls." And he left.

The knots inside my stomach had loosened up, too. Dad was okay. And he knew that the garage was our territory. And he'd probably be working soon, anyway. Things were going okay.

We got through the play three times before lunch. Katie was our audience. At first she acted surprised when we asked her how it looked. People didn't usually ask Katie's advice on things. But after a while, she perked up and started volunteering criticism. Interrupting us, even.

"Hold the dinosaur up more, Erin. Your arms are showing, Heather. I can't hear the cave girl's voice too well."

By the end of the third practice, my shoulder muscles were ready to cave in.

102

"That's it. I can't told my arms up one more second."

"Let's go get the Kool-Aid, then."

Things were falling into place. Even the grocery store cooperated. We couldn't believe our luck when we saw the package of paper cups with wild animal pictures all over them, and "Jungle Safari" printed on the box.

"They ordered them just for us," I said solemnly.

The Ara Project was working. The garage looked perfect, the show was almost ready. And Heather had printed my name next to hers on her camp registration form, then sealed it before her Mom saw the change. I had written a note to the clinic, asking them to please send my health record to Camp Firefly; I'd printed the address neatly on an envelope, so they would be sure to send it to the right place. There wouldn't be any problems. I hadn't seen a doctor in four years, and that showed just how healthy I was.

We ate lunch at her house. It was Heather's idea, not her mom's, who was trying to keep up with all the people at her rummage sale. And more cars kept driving up.

"Come to the Jungle Day tomorrow!" we called to all the kids. "It's four blocks over, on Cherry Street. There's going to be a puppet show! Jungle Potion Punch! A rope swing and lots more!" Katie held the sign in one hand and her sandwich in the other.

"I can hardly wait until tomorrow!" Heather almost hugged me good-bye, she was so excited. "I'll bring more pitchers tomorrow. It's going to be perfect!"

I smiled all the way home—until I turned the corner and saw the smoke coming thick and black out of the chimney.

Nineteen

◨◨◨

Our jungle branches were blazing away in the fireplace; Dad was sprawled on the couch, slack, red-faced; the living room was an oven.

I hate fires. They are ugly and hot and *wrong* when it's eighty-five degrees outside. And I hate bottles. Ugly long green bottles spread all over the table. And I hate promises. And the stupid people who believe them; believe even for a moment that things will really be different. They never were. I wouldn't fall for that line ever again.

I ran into the kitchen with Katie close behind. Geri turned around from the stove.

"I didn't see him go into the garage, Erin. And he didn't get all the branches. Really. I checked."

I just looked at her. I *knew* it would happen. Maybe he did just get a few today, but what about tomorrow, the day of the show, when all those kids were around? I didn't even try to talk over the big lump in my throat.

Geri pushed a sticky green Rice Krispies mash out of the saucepan into a cake pan and patted it level. "These are for you and Heather. I put some green food coloring in. Like the jungle, you know.

You can serve them with your punch." She handed the spatula to Katie to lick. "My contribution to Jungle Day. You can call them, uh . . . I know! Tarzan's Treats." She grinned. She was trying to cheer me up.

"We *won't* call them that!" But then I changed my tone when I saw the hurt look on her face. "Thanks, Geri, they'll really help us make money. I just don't like that name." I tried to smile. "How about Jungle Jumbos?"

Mom didn't look a bit surprised to see him on the couch when she came home from work. Just grim. Dinner was very quiet. Too quiet, like the air right before a thunderstorm.

There wasn't any fight after dinner. But, even so, I couldn't get to sleep. My room was too hot. And there was a sour feeling in my stomach, reaching almost to my throat. I got up finally to get a drink.

I stopped outside my door. Dad was making his way down the hall, holding onto the wall. His steps were heavy, unsteady. His hair stuck out, his shirt was stained, and his eyes were bleary, red, half-open.

I didn't want to be anywhere near him, didn't want to even look at him, all dirty and smelly and stumbling. I took a step backward.

He lurched near my door. "Wasa matter?" he mumbled, squinting at me.

I tried to make my face go blank. But tonight things were too wrong. The disappointed, betrayed feeling was curdling from deep inside. I felt my face muscles tighten, felt my lips curl, felt the anger and

106

contempt flow from my face, my eyes, my whole body. And then I heard the words. Words I'd never said out loud before. They came out of their own will, low and bitter.

"You're *drunk*. That's what's the matter!"

His head jerked up a little. He blinked, as if he was really trying to focus, to pull it all together. His expression changed from the sullen angry look to— something else. Baffled, perplexed almost. Like he was trying hard to make sense of my words.

I shut my mouth. But the words were already gone. A tingly unreal feeling buzzed through me. I took another step back. That look—on his face—

But then another voice shot down the hall. Sharp, disgusted: "Get to bed before you fall on the floor."

Mom was standing at the other end of the hall, very straight, eyes flashing, watching him, watching me.

Dad turned to her. The fumbling look on his face changed back to a scowl. "Gotahell," he muttered. He took three more steps, reeling toward the bedroom, and slammed the door.

And then there were just Mom and me left in the hot stuffy hall. I bit my lip. I was shaking. The hallway was turning into a watery blur. I started to run back to my room.

But Mom's hand was on my arm. "Erin, wait." She stayed beside me, walking to my room, helping me into bed like I was Katie; then, just sitting there a minute, at the edge of the bed.

107

"Erin—" She paused, as if she was trying to make up her mind. She looked at me with those eyes that always saw right through everything. She pushed a strand of hair off my forehead.

"Erin—" Her voice was gentle, but firm, too. "He's not a very good one, I know, but remember—he is still your father."

The house was still hot in the morning. I was surprised to hear Mrs. Morris's voice when I walked in the kitchen. She and Mom were standing on the back porch, talking.

"Well, I better scoot home now, or you'll miss your bus to work." Mrs. Morris's voice floated in through the back door. Then, in a lower tone that I could barely hear, "Now remember—I meant what I said. If there's any way that Doug and I can help—"

"Thank you." The rest of Mom's answer was lost as the two of them started down the driveway.

There was a plate of muffins on the table. I picked one up and turned it around and around in my hand. I made my eyes focus on it—not on the bedroom down the hall, where Dad was sleeping. I stared at the muffin until it seemed to grow three sizes bigger.

"Today is Jungle Day," I told the muffin. "Think about *that*—nothing else." And I chomped down hard on it—green specks and all.

Dad stayed in his room, sleeping. I didn't even look down that end of the hall. I wouldn't think about him.

"It's supposed to get to ninety. I hope you made lots of punch," Geri said, walking into the kitchen. "That's what'll make money today."

Our show was set for one o'clock. Heather brought over two pitchers and more packets of Kool-Aid at eleven.

It was hard to tell who was more excited, Heather or Katie. Katie was everywhere I turned, all morning, until I finally put her to work making one more sign. And Heather was as bouncy as a Slinky toy. "By tonight we'll be rich, Erin!"

"Right." But I didn't share her excitement at all. My nervous feeling was more like before a dentist appointment. Dad hadn't come out yet. What would happen when he did? Did he have bottles in there with him? Each time I looked over at the house, my stomach took a little jump. I could hardly wait for one o'clock to come, so I could get the whole thing over with.

Geri was right. Our jungle potion was a big hit. Almost before we got the table set up we had three kids waiting.

"Fifteen cents a glass," I told them.

"Should be a dime." It was Jay, from down the street. "They're such dinky cups."

"They're *jungle* cups!" Heather glared at him.

"So what's all that about?" He pointed to the sign that Katie just hung.

"Our puppet show. And jungle room. Real jungle scenery and a rope swing ride." I thought I sounded very businesslike.

109

"Only seventy-five cents," Heather added.

"You're kidding!" He laughed. A rude, germy laugh, right into our pitcher. "Seventy-five cents for some dumb puppet show." He threw his cup on the grass and walked off.

"A lot you know!" I yelled after him. But I was worried. Was our price too high?

By twelve-thirty, we had sold four of our six pitchers of Kool-Aid and all of Geri's Rice Krispies bars, which really weren't so jumbo, because we cut them small to make more money. But only four little kids hung around for the show.

Heather was getting worried, too. "When something doesn't sell at Mom's rummage sale, she marks the price down," she said, chewing a strand of hair. "I know." She yanked the sign down and turned it over. "I'll make it sound like a real bargain."

Jungle Show Special: Today only. Includes
Free Glass of Jungle Potion and Free Ride
on Dangerous Swing.   50¢

"But it's not dangerous!"

"For little kids it is." She wiped her hands together. "That ought to do it."

It helped. By one o'clock we had a dozen kids wandering through the garage, swinging, feeling the doo-dels and the fishnet web and the snake that was swimming around in dark colored water so no one could tell he was a manicotti noodle.

I looked back at the house for one last time before I got behind our cardboard theater. So far,

110

so good. Maybe all my nervousness was because of the play. I pulled on my puppet.

Just then Katie's head poked around the corner. "Erin—" She looked at Heather and bit her lip.

"Katie, get out of here! We're starting!" I could have clobbered her.

"Erin—" Her voice squeaked. "Daddy's coming. I saw him through the window. And he's wobbly. . . ."

"Get Geri, quick!" I shut my eyes for a second. The dread was closing over my head like deep water. I had waited all day for it to happen, and here it was. Nothing I could do now.

The next fifteen minutes were like trying to listen to two radio stations at the same time and not keeping track of either one. Puppets on stage—and Katie and Geri and Dad outside somewhere. Would Katie get Geri in time? Would Geri be able to keep Dad away from our show? Had the other kids noticed? Did he look really drunk? My head started pounding.

Heather rammed me with her elbow. She was babbling about something that was completely ad-lib, because I'd never even heard it before. She rammed me again. I must have missed my cue.

"It is I, Pella, girl of Pellucidar!" I cried. Heather groaned. Wrong line.

It wasn't fair. After all the work of getting ready for the show, to have it go by like this in a big blur of mixed-up lines. But we bungled along, until Philip and his dad finished exploring Pellucidar and got safely back to their own world.

111

It was a wonderful relief to drop my aching arms and pull off the puppets after the last scene. But my head didn't feel any better.

"Was it awful?" I whispered.

Heather groaned. "You made the mountain growl instead of," she started giggling, "instead of Tyrannosaurus! But the kids are clapping out there. Maybe they like comedies."

My legs had gone completely to sleep. I stood up slowly, took a deep breath, and walked out from behind the stage.

Katie was standing very straight and tall by the rope swing. "Your turn," she told a little boy who was just an inch shorter than she was. "Everybody else wait by the wall." Her squeaky little voice sounded very prim and proper.

I had to grin. That was probably the first time in her whole life that Katie was in charge of anything or anybody. She didn't look upset, or worried about Dad. Was everything okay, then?

Geri was standing by the door, next to the punch table. While I watched, she poured two kids their jungle potion, then went back by the door.

She had made him leave, somehow. And she was standing guard by the door. I suddenly wanted to run over and hug her. But instead I limped over on pins-and-needles legs and poured some jungle potion. "How was the show? Did we do okay?"

"It looked kind of mixed-up to me. But I only saw the last part." Our eyes met. She nodded slightly. An "it's okay" nod.

112

"Thanks," I said, twisting my cup around and around. The evil tarmangani hadn't crashed our show after all. And those little kids in the audience wouldn't have understood our plot anyway, so it didn't matter that we'd goofed it up.

It was three o'clock by the time the last kid finished his last swing and gulped the last sugary drops from the punch.

"Done," Heather said. We looked at each other.

"Ready, set—"

"*Go!*" We both dived for the coffee can. Nickels, dimes, pennies, quarters poured onto the floor. We had a whole mountain of coins, but was it enough to bring forty-two dollars up to eighty-five?

"Be enough. Be almost enough," I whispered, separating out the quarters. Heather took the dimes. Then came the nickels. The pennies took forever.

"Seventy-eight, seventy-nine, eighty," I mumbled.

"Sh, you're making me lose count."

Finally we had the copper piles lined up beside the silvery ones. And we added up the piles. Twice, just to be sure.

"Fourteen dollars and fifty-five cents." I poured it through my hand back into the coffee can.

"Almost fifteen dollars!"

"Not bad. . . ."

"What do you mean, not bad! We're rich!" She grabbed the rope and swung clear across the garage, while I did more math. Forty-two plus almost fifteen came to fifty-seven dollars. I still needed twenty-

113

eight. We'd made a lot. But now I just had my birthday to count on. Twenty-eight dollars was a lot of money. Aunt Jeanne never sent that much.

Something else was wrong, too. I tossed Mom's three quarters around in my palm.

"You know, Heather, half of all this money is yours."

She slid right off her rope and put her hands on her hips. Her eyes got that steely cat-gleam.

"It's all *Ara* money! For you and me to spend a week together at camp. I won't even know the other campers, and for sure they won't know about E.R.B. It's for me, too! I won't have any fun, if you can't come."

Just then Katie skipped up. Her mouth was all jungle potion and smiles. "I'm rich, too," she said. She pointed to an empty fishline hanging from the rafter.

"A little boy wanted it, so I sold my doo-del!"

Twenty

◧◧◧

There was smoke coming out of the chimney when I left the garage. But today it wasn't such a shock. Today I didn't have to worry about my jungle branches going into the fireplace. I went in through the back door with my coffee can of riches.

"We made almost fifteen dollars. Thanks for making the cookies. They went fast." I splashed cold water from the sink on my face. "That garage is *hot*. What's for dinner?"

"I don't know—now." Geri's voice was low, angry. I looked up in surprise.

"What's the matter?"

The front door opened. Mom's shoes clicked across the house. Her steps sounded mad already. She'd seen Dad right away. And the fire.

Geri stood up. "Guess I better tell her the good news."

"What?" I asked again. Just then Mom walked in. Geri opened the kitchen cupboards.

"Look," she said, pointing. One whole shelf, the canned goods shelf, was empty. "See?" she said to Mom.

Mom stared.

"That— He took them back. *Sold* them back."
She grabbed the plastic dishpan and started the cold
water running, hard.

I looked at Geri. I felt shaky all over. What was
Mom doing?

Geri's eyes were wide. "Mom, do you think you
should. . . ."

"He sold back our food," Mom said. She lifted
the full dishpan and started for the living room,
holding it in front of her, like a weapon. I followed,
slowly.

She stood over him a full minute, then dumped
the whole pan of water on his head. Water whooshed
all over everything.

He jerked up, wide-awake, and grabbed her
wrist. "What'd you do that for!"

"Let go of me, you drunk." And in a very loud
calm voice, "Geri, stay here. Erin, get Mr. Morris.
Right now."

Mom's face was cold, hard. Dad looked completely sober, completely furious. I ran. My insides
were shaking like jello, and my ears were buzzing.
My bare feet, slapping the sidewalk, were a long way
from my fuzzy head.

The Morrises understood right away. Mr.
Morris was out the door as soon as my story was half
told. I started to follow him, but Mrs. Morris put
her arm on my shoulder and pulled me back into the
kitchen.

"You stay right here now, Erin. They'll take
care of things over there." Her voice was firm and
friendly at the same time. She set a glass of milk in

116

front of me, like I was Katie, just back from kindergarten. "Everything will work out now; you calm down. Have a cookie, Erin. Where's Katie?"

I didn't know where Katie was. I didn't know anything. I wanted to go home, and I wanted to stay here with her clucking over me like a mother hen, saying, "They'll take care of things; it'll be all right." I reached for my milk and realized for the first time that I was still holding my coffee can. I felt like an idiot.

Five minutes later, Mr. Morris's car pulled away, with Dad in it. I wondered where Mr. Morris was taking him. Back to jail?

"I think your mom will want you home now, Erin. Here, bring some cookies to Katie and Geri."

Katie had been in the garage, thank goodness, packing up her doo-dels. I peeked in the front door before I let her go in with me.

The fire in the fireplace had burned out completely. The window was open as wide as it would go. The couch cushions were up on end, drying out. Mom was sitting in the armchair, very straight and still. "We're airing the place out," she said grimly. "For good."

"What happened?" I whispered to Geri, when Mom was out of the room.

"Mr. Morris was really great," she whispered back. "He got Dad all calmed down. Dad thought Mr. Morris was on *his* side."

"But where did they go?"

"Probably downtown. To one of those cheap apartments or hotel rooms. Dad's stayed in them before." She lowered her voice even more. "And he was so mad at Mom he *wanted* to leave."

I think dinner was cheese sandwiches. Afterward I went straight to my room. The attic was an oven, but there was work to do. I sat on my wooden plank, under the light bulb, and chewed on my pen.

Jungle Day had taken a lot of my time and thoughts the past few weeks. Now Bal-Za, Golden Girl, lost daughter of Tarzan, needed my help badly. And I needed her. It was time to get back to her. Her first night in the dark jungle would be terrifying. Eyes glittering at her out of the darkness, strange noises. Sheeta? Numa?

I shuddered along with her. I couldn't leave her there, alone and unprotected, even though she was trying hard to brave the dangers. Tarzan had to be alerted somehow. He had to come to her rescue. I wrote rapidly. Tarzan, her father, was swinging through the vine trails, following the whispers of the jungle animals, whispers that only he could understand. They told Tarzan that there was a girl lost in the jungle, a girl with long hair the color of Kudu's light. Tarzan moved swiftly through the jungle heights, hurtling from vine to vine, trying to pick up the scent-spoor of his daughter. Hoping that it was she, and that he was not too late.

Twenty-One

Geri came running into my room at six thirty the next morning.

"Mom's nose is bleeding." She shook me awake. "It's been bleeding a long time; we can't get it to stop. She has to go to the hospital."

"What!" I was wide awake and out of bed the next second. Mom was sitting in the bathroom with her head back and a big handkerchief up against her nose. It was supposed to be a white handkerchief, but it was red. And there was blood on the floor, in the sink, and all over her hands and clothes. She sat there, white and quiet.

"Mom!"

"It's *all right*." Her voice was low and muffled, through the cloth. "Just a nosebleed. The doctors will fix me up in no time."

I heard voices in the living room. And then Mrs. Morris hurried down the hall. "Don't you worry, now; we'll get you up to the hospital in no time."

Geri rushed out of her bedroom, belting up her good slacks. She was going along—

"Wait, I'm coming too," I called, heading for my room. But Geri grabbed me.

119

"No. Someone has to watch Katie. You'd just have to wait in the lobby, anyway. You're not old enough." She ran after Mom and Mrs. Morris. The front door slammed.

The house was too empty, after that. I prowled around like Numa in a cage, waiting for the call from the hospital. It's just a nosebleed, I told myself over and over. Nosebleeds aren't so bad. Kids at school just go to the nurse's office until it stops. So Mom would be home soon.

But that's not what Geri said when she finally called.

"Mom has to stay in the hospital. Her blood pressure is way too high, and the nosebleed isn't stopping. She might need a transfusion."

"A what?"

"More blood. She's lost a lot. Mrs. Morris is bringing me home. I have to pack some of Mom's things."

Katie sat on the couch with her blanket all the long morning.

"Can't you think of anything else to do?" I said finally. "Go watch TV or go outside. Do something!"

She just sat there with that rag of a blanket. "I don't want Mommy to be sick in the hospital!" She started to cry.

"Katie, Mom probably won't be there long. And —and—" I tried to think of something to cheer her up. Why wasn't Geri here? What good was she doing at the hospital all day?

"I know, Katie. You can make a card for Mom. A get-well card."

She drew a person with a sad face. Then she drew a house as big as the person. Next came the sun and moon and stars. Grass, flowers, some kind of animal with horns. . . .

"Very good, Katie," Geri said, when she finally got back. "Mom will really like that." And she flopped full length on the cushionless couch. "What a day," she said with a long sigh. "Mom's got to stay there for a while, and I'm in charge while she's gone."

Katie waved her card over Geri's face. "What should my card say? Write some words!"

"Later."

"Write some words now!" Her voice trembled.

Geri groaned and sat up. She grabbed the pencil and doodled a minute. Then her mouth twitched a little; she started writing. I watched over her shoulder.

"Everybloody Knose we miss you." She flopped back down with a smug grin. "How's that?"

"Cute," I said. "Very cute."

But I did miss her. The next day was even worse. It should have helped to hear Mom's voice on the phone when she called.

"That card was so clever. It really cheered me up. Cute picture, too. And that saying! Who thought it up?"

"Geri."

"Erin, so much has happened these past few days. I've been lying here just now and thinking that I never even asked you how your big Jungle Day went."

121

"We did really great. We made fifteen dollars almost." The coffee can was in my attic. I hadn't thought much about it since the nosebleed.

"I'm really sorry I missed your big show. I would have liked to have seen it. Maybe you can give me a special performance when I get home." Her voice was thinning out, losing its bounce. "Put Katie on, would you?"

She liked the card. Clever slogan. That was Geri's. She liked the picture. That was Katie's. I should have made her something. I was as clever as they were. Who made Jungle Day happen, anyway?

Jungle Day. The words hung at the edge of my brain, like an idea almost hatched. What had Mom said? That she wanted a *special* performance?

The idea sprouted then, full and bright and perfect, like an Ara flash. I could cheer Mom up, too.

Twenty-Two

□□□

"**S**he's on the second floor. We have to get up there fast. If we pass anyone, look official."

"Second floor." Heather groaned. She pulled the white sheet tighter around our flattened theater. "With *this*? Lucky thing for you my mom knows the head of the hospital auxiliary." She pointed to her pink and white candy striper apron. "We wouldn't have had a chance without these. I told Mom we needed them for a play." She giggled. "No lie!"

"Just so long as no one asks us to push patients around or anything." I locked my fingers under the bag of puppets and props. "The hard part will be finding Mom's room. Two ten."

Heather shook her head. "This is the nerviest thing you ever dreamed up, Erin Callahan."

"This way, hurry." I kept my head high, hoping my bag looked like medicines or bandages.

Not a soul on the stairway. So far, so good. 222–220–218. . . .

A nurse walked by, looking down at her charts. I shoved my bag to one side, so my candy striper apron showed. She gave us a quick glance and kept walking.

"Passed checkpoint one," Heather hissed.

216–214–212–210.

"Hi, Mom," I whispered, peeking around the door. I felt like a secret agent.

Her eyes flew open. "How did you—" And then, as we both slipped in and shut the door, "You aren't—"

"You said you wanted a special performance," I said, with a grin of pure triumph, and opened up the stage.

"We now present for your enjoyment: *Pellucidar: World Inside the Earth.*"

Philip came on stage, speaking in his almost-English accent.

"This land that Father and I have found is savage and wild. Who would have dreamed that such a prehistoric jungle exists inside our earth!"

Tyrannosaurus rose up above the mountain, with fierce noises.

"A dinosaur! I am trapped!"

Enter native girl, Pella. "Who is that strange boy standing there so stupidly? The great monster will devour him."

I made her voice loud and dramatic. And I held the mountain tall with my other hand. This was fun! Not at all like the time in the garage, when I was so nervous about Dad I didn't even know what I was doing. This time I could feel the excitement and drama, romping the puppets through the wild and harrowing dangers of Pellucidar, until the final heart-rending scene, where the explorers returned to earth

124

in their makeshift basket. Geri wasn't the only one with acting talent!

Heather yanked on the string to raise the basket above the stage. But it didn't go up.

"Pull again," I hissed, too loud.

"I *am* pulling. It won't go."

There was a chuckle from outside the stage. It didn't sound like Mom. Maybe her roommate was enjoying the poor stuck basket.

Heather gave one last desperate yank; the basket pulled free, nearly spilling out the puppets, then sailed out of sight over the theater.

"Darn basket," Heather muttered. Then she clapped me on the back, puppet and all. "You were great! I was great! The play was great!"

I rubbed my shoulder. "Did you ever hold up a papier-mâché mountain for ten whole minutes nonstop?"

Then we stared at each other. There was clapping from outside the stage. More clapping than two pairs of hands could do.

I peered around the theater.

Mom and her roommate—an elderly lady— were sitting up in their beds, grinning and clapping. Beside them were two nurses and an orderly. And in the doorway, a wheelchair patient. And behind him —a doctor.

Twenty-Three

"**W**e should have charged!" Heather's face was one big grin. "They loved it! They would have paid the whole seventy-five cents, even without the swing ride!"

I grinned back. All our training in denizen skills had paid off. We'd penetrated the very depths of the hospital halls. We were a success, a smashing success. *Now* Mom knew who was clever.

"You know those singing telegrams that people send?" I giggled. "Well, this was our dramagram. From Pellucidar!"

But the word telegram remained me of letters, as in Aunt Jeanne and birthday. Neither of us had mentioned Jungle Day, the coffee can, or Camp Firefly yet today. Mom's nosebleed and hospital stay were like a cover on top of all that. Our project was still there, still top secret, still *vital*, as these last days ticked away. But for right now, Ara was in hiding, like the coffee can, while we waited for my birthday money and for Mom to get better.

She was supposed to come home the next morning. But a nosebleed at nine a.m. changed that plan and kept her there the rest of the day and the next. My birthday.

Because Mom arranged it all through the right people, I was allowed a visit on my birthday. This time I marched right in the front door and up to her room without any candy striper camouflage.

I brought two things: a bunch of flowers from Mrs. Morris's garden, and a picture pamphlet about Camp Firefly in my pocket. It was time at last to bring the Ara Project out of hiding.

"Well, come in, Puppeteer! Happy Birthday!"

Mom looked nice. Her dark hair was brushed and shiny, and she was wearing a pretty nightgown. There was a big plastic bag full of yarn beside her, and a little package wrapped in tissue. She looked more relaxed than I'd seen her in a long time.

"I wanted to be home to celebrate your birthday properly, Erin. But around here, what the doctor says, goes."

I sat down carefully on the smoothed bed. "Did he tell you why your nose keeps bleeding?"

"Well, you see, the body has its own warning system, when you're not treating it right. And I was worrying a lot and working a lot, like an old biddy hen. I worried my blood pressure way up into the danger zone. The nosebleeds were the safety valve, you could say. So the doctor wants me to take it easy for a while. Anyway," and she shoved the tissue package at me. "This is the best I can do for now. Happy birthday."

It was soft and squishy, but too small to be clothes. The tissue paper came off easily. I stared down at—

A puppet. A crocheted puppet. A green dinosaur crocheted puppet, with white pointed teeth and dark green scales and a very red open mouth, and wicked eyes, with lids.

I looked from the puppet to the yarn bag to Mom. "I didn't know you could crochet something like this!"

She looked pleased. "Well, I haven't exactly had the time to sit around these past few months. But I used to crochet a lot. I made Katie's blanket five years ago, you know. That dirty old rag was once a beautiful popcorn stitch. Mrs. Morris brought me the yarn for Tyrannosaurus here."

I tried it on. "It moves a lot easier than papier-mâché! Can you crochet mountains, too?" I giggled.

Puppets. Jungle Day. Camp Firefly. My pamphlet was still tucked into my back pocket. "Now," said a tiny voice inside me. "Bring it out now; explain what you want for your *real* present."

I started to open my mouth. But just then Mom leaned back against the pillow and shut her eyes for a minute.

"Erin, this hospital rest has given me time to really think things through. It's also caused some surprising things to happen. That's what I want to talk to you about. It's part of your birthday present, too."

I leaned forward. She hadn't already bought something! She couldn't have.

If she knew how hard I was listening and how tense I was, she would have gotten right to the point. But she didn't know. And she got philosophical instead.

128

"You rush around like a chicken with its head cut off, trying to work problems out your own way. Then, when it seems like the rug has been completely pulled out from under your feet and you can't possibly do another thing, suddenly things shape up. And the pieces do fit together after all, but in a whole different pattern."

I listened politely. I was glad that the new puzzle pattern, whatever it was, made her so relaxed and calm. But what did it have to do with my birthday?

". . . like the house," she was saying, "and the car." She looked at me. "Do you remember the elderly lady in the bed next to me, Erin? She had to go into a convalescent home."

I bounced a little on the bed. I'd hardly noticed the other patient and I certainly didn't care to hear about an old lady's troubles.

"Her family is helping her sell a lot of things, including her car. It's eighteen years old, but it runs." Mom leaned back further on the pillow.

"The price is so low, she's practically giving it away. I can't pass up this chance when we need a car so badly. But until we sell the house, we'll have to scrape for every penny we can get to pay her. It's only fair to her to pay right away, in cash."

The dinosaur's head flopped into a nosedive. So did my whole brain. The dread oozed out all the way to my fingertips and toes. Oh no. It wasn't fair. It wasn't fair. Not when it was so *close*. Only twenty-eight dollars left to pay. And not even that much when Aunt Jeanne's envelope came. And not on my—

129

"Birthday present, a big one. And for all of us. Better than an outfit or a game, Erin. Just think what we can do with a car again."

So who needed a car? Tarzan didn't need one, or Korak, or Bal-Za. They could go anywhere they wanted on their own muscle power. It was a dumb tarmangani machine, and it was *going to wreck all my plans*!

"And that's not all." Mom went on and on. More wonderful puzzle pieces. Heather's own mother was the traitor this time. She had come to visit Mom last night. She knew a young couple who were looking for an older house just like ours. She'd be sure to tell them ours was up for sale.

I sat there while Mom's new jigsaw smashed my puzzle pieces everywhere: my attic, my camp plans, everything. She didn't *understand*. I had to do something.

Nothing was for certain yet. The car wasn't bought. The money wasn't spent. I had the camp pamphlet right here in my pocket. If she saw those beautiful trees and lake, she'd see why I needed the money. And she'd see how hard I'd already worked. She'd understand. She'd say, "Oh, I see, Erin. Yes, certainly. The car can wait." All I had to do was tell her.

"So I'll take the doctor's advice and not think about anything except what flavor of birthday cake you want when I come home. No more worrying for now."

"Everybloody Knose we miss you." And if I made her change it all, make her feel bad and start worrying again, she wouldn't be coming home; her nose would overflow again.

Right now it was my eyes that were going to overflow, any second. Because, watching Mom sitting so relaxed and smiling in that bed, I knew that the pamphlet of Camp Firefly was going to stay in my pocket, and I was going to stay at home next week. I knew it with a hot burning throat and a tight hurting head. I wanted to reach into my pocket and throw down the pamphlet. But I didn't. I didn't do anything to give away the very secret, very dead Ara Project.

Instead I stood up and said in a gulpy voice: "I want chocolate, and—don't get any more nosebleeds!" And I ran out of the room.

Twenty-Four

□□□

There was birthday mail waiting at home. One was a card from Dad. It said in neat backhand script:

> Erin, my fondest wishes for your twelfth birthday. I hope you receive everything your heart desires.
>
> > Yours truly,
> > Dad
>
> P.S. I haven't forgotten the dress

The return address was 111 Main Street, Apartment 11. All those number ones meant he was living in one of the old rundown apartments down the street from Joe's. The card also meant that he had a job, at least when he bought it, and that he was sober, at least when he wrote it. I'd gotten letters from him before, when he was living away from home. They were always formal and polite, just like this one. Very different from the way he really talked.

"I haven't forgotten the dress." I bit my lip, thinking back to that awful night in the hall, and

those hateful words. *My* words. "You're *drunk.*"
And that look on his face—

I held the card tightly. The dress didn't matter.
But I was glad to get the card, glad that he'd been
too drunk to remember that night, glad that he still
wanted to send "fondest wishes."

The other mail was from Aunt Jeanne, in a
box, not an envelope. A small box, with a silver
charm bracelet and a four-leaf clover charm on it.
"Erin, I thought I'd send something different for
once, something more personal than money."

I clenched my fists, hard. Get a hold of yourself,
Erin Callahan. You already knew you weren't going
to Camp Firefly. What if this box had come before
the talk with Mom, when you were still hoping? This
way it doesn't matter so much, because you can't feel
any worse.

Right. I couldn't feel any worse.

Mom came home on Friday and lay around re-
cuperating and making lots of telephone arrangements all weekend. And I hung around like a . . .
well, what was the name for the opposite of ghost?
For a body that was just blank where the inside feeling part should be?

Heather wasn't numb. She was mad, really mad
on the phone Friday night. "If there's no way to get
the money in time, then I won't go either. It's the
two of us together."

I didn't know how to explain that there was no
use fighting it; that it wasn't just money anymore. It
was blood pressure and all kinds of things mixed

133

together. Heather's mom was always so healthy and busy with projects. Heather wouldn't understand.

She was even angrier on the phone the next night.

"Erin, I think they *want* to get rid of me! Mom got so upset, you wouldn't believe it! She went on and on about how all the money's been paid and I don't appreciate how lucky I am, and how she and Dad had plans, anyway. It's their vacation, too."

She was Sabora, lion-girl, growling. It probably didn't happen too often that she set her heart on something and then didn't get it.

Maybe it was because I had just had a birthday, but suddenly I felt older than her. I knew, and she didn't. No ranting or raving would help. It was— meant to be, that's all. Might as well take it with jungle stoicism.

"I'll keep the coffee can safe in the attic," I said in the most steady voice I could manage. "We can divide it up later." I didn't say anything so dumb as "Have a good time," or, "See you next week."

Monday Mom went back to work. Monday Heather and her mom left for Camp Firefly. Monday the numbness started wearing off, like Novocaine after a filling. All afternoon I kept seeing Heather's mom's blue Nissan pull into the campground. I cried that night, with my face stuffed into my pillow.

On Tuesday I thought about the lake and wondered if Heather was swimming or boating or fishing. I tried to picture the trees. Did they really have high swinging places, like Tarzan used? And was Heather climbing high into the jungle reaches? If there was a way to get up there, Heather would find it. She made things happen; right now she was making them happen up north, without me. It wasn't fair.

Tuesday night Mom drove home from work in an old car with rust spots all over it.

"It's ours," she announced as she got out, all smiles. "I know it's not exactly the latest model, but it has four wheels, and an engine and a steering wheel."

"A car!" Geri yelped. She was across the lawn and in the car in two seconds flat. "A real honest-to-goodness car! Give me the keys, please," she practically sang out the window to Mom.

"Have you driven a stick shift before?"

"Oh dear." Geri stared at the gearshift. "The driver's ed cars at school were automatic. So was Mona's when I went for my driver's license."

"Then let's just take it around the block, slowly, for a starter." Mom slid in and waved at me. "Come on, Erin. You and Katie climb in the back. "We're going for our first spin in our new car."

Geri jiggled the gearshift lightly. "Hmmm . . . I suppose that extra pedal is supposed to do something, right?"

"It's the clutch," Mom explained. "And you need it before you switch gears or brake. Got it?" She leaned over and showed Geri the gearshift positions and how to use the clutch.

"Remember, ease off the clutch with your left foot as you press down on the gas with your right."

135

"Clutch, gas, left foot, right foot," Geri mumbled, hunched over the wheel. "No problem." But her voice didn't sound too confident.

She turned the key and tried to work the pedals. On her first try the engine died. On her second try, Mom yelled, "Not like that! You'll strip the gears!" On her third try, the car started moving.

"Hang on everyone!" Geri yelled. "I think I've got it!" And we took off like a frog down the road. Lurch, bump, stop—first gear. Lurch, jerk stop—second gear. Lurch, shudder, *zoom*—third gear. She swerved around the corner, tumbling me and Katie into a heap.

"Just like the tilt-a-whirl!" Katie cried.

"Geri! Slow down!"

"This is a wonderful car!" Geri cried, sitting straight and tall at the wheel. "She has *personality*. She needs a name!"

"How about Captain Kangaroo?" I suggested.

"I've got it!" Geri gave the dashboard a whack. "Matilda the Second. This car has the same free independent spirit as our old Matilda, only *this* one has wheels. She can really go places! Matilda reincarnated!"

"Well, if a cat can have nine lives, why not a washing machine," Mom said, laughing. We swerved around another corner in third gear, and her voice changed. "Geri. This is a car, not a toy, remember?"

But it might as well have been Geri's toy. She played with it nonstop the rest of the week.

"Erin, would you clean up the breakfast dishes?" she'd ask, popping her head around the corner and jingling the car keys, "I'm taking Mom to work so I can use the car today."

"Erin, you stay here with Katie a few minutes. I'm taking the car around the block a few times to practice shifting."

"Erin, I'm going to pick up Mom. Will you fry the hamburgers tonight?"

It was very clear to me whose birthday present the car really was.

Thursday was the worst day. All day long I thought about the fireworks show Heather had told me about. We had planned to watch it together, from a high tree.

I tried to work on Bal-Za to make the time pass. Bal-Za needed to find her father. Her story needed to get finished. But the jungle feeling was as far away as Camp Firefly or Jungle Africa. The story wouldn't come.

I climbed down from the attic and stood by my bedroom window. Warm breeze, dark sky, fireflies. Little yellow blinks of light all over the yard. Off and on. Off and on. Watching them gave my stomach a pinched feeling. They were blinking on purpose, just to make me feel bad.

Little Ara bugs in the sky tonight. And tomorrow, Friday, July fourth, there would be huge rocket lights. At Camp Firefly, the fireworks would be right over the lake. Would Heather still find a high boma tree to watch it from, even without me?

My nose clogged up and my eyes blurred, so that the little firefly lights got long and watery. Firefly, fireworks, camp, boma, Bal-Za. The words shook around in my head like a kaleidoscope, with greens for the jungle, and blues for the water, and yellow for the fireflies.

And then the picture cleared. I saw it all in one swift flash. For the first time all week, my brain started moving. Slow at first, like Matilda the Second, then faster, until I worked out the whole thing.

I wasn't going to sit up here in my hot bedroom tomorrow, while the fireworks lit the sky. I wasn't going to arrange Bal-Za's final thrilling reunion with Tarzan from my bedroom, like a director offstage. I wasn't going to stay home feeling sorry for myself one more day, while Geri cruised all over town.

I was going camping, too.

Twenty-Five

□□□

Loud talking floated out the window of Maddens Restaurant. The tarmangani were clinking glasses, laughing, getting an early start on Fourth of July celebrations.

It was a bad time to climb the willow. But I had waited all day, with my backpack hidden under my bed. The chance hadn't come until thirty minutes ago, when Mom and Geri and Katie went to the store for sparklers. In the car, of course.

I left a note on the kitchen table. It said, "Sharon Knudson invited me to watch fireworks at the park with her and spend the night. I'll walk home tomorrow."

Mom would believe that. I used to do things with Sharon a lot, before Heather and I got so busy with E.R.B. and the boma. Mom might be mad that I didn't ask first. But I could worry about that tomorrow.

Yes, a bad time to climb. But I was a trained denizen. I knew how to melt into the shadows, crawling out over the roof, then down onto the boma. Safe.

I pulled out my supplies. A beach towel to lie on, two cans of pop, one bologna sandwich, a box of chocolate chip cookies, my Bal-Za notebook and pen,

Son of Tarzan, a flashlight, and my jackknife. Everything I needed to camp out under the stars and watch the fireworks from my own hidden boma.

Summer had changed the willow since I'd last been here with Heather. The leaves had lost that fresh gold-green shininess. They were darker, ragged-edged, and scabbed from the insects. But they still swept down over the roof like long trailing jungle vines, still arched across the river, still hid the boma from the eyes of the tarmangani.

Other things were different, too. Like the slant of Kudu's rays, and the slightly foul smell from the river. And the air was thicker, buggier, buzzier.

I wanted to tell Heather about the changes. Only trained jungle senses would appreciate them. I even opened my mouth, then shut it. Of course Heather wasn't here. She was up north. And for the first time ever, I was alone in the boma; as alone as if I was truly in jungle Africa.

It didn't matter. Korak had been alone. And Tarzan. They had hunted and learned jungle ways. Well, I had things to do, too. A sandwich to eat, and pop and cookies; chapters to read and write.

It took Kudu a very long time to slide down in the western sky. Twilight hung around him in the clouds, golden and quiet. Behind him, the sky colors went from blue to pink to purple. The water got darker and farther away. The buzzes got louder around my head, my arms, my legs.

I stretched out on the towel with my flashlight and book, but my eyes kept watching the shadows instead of the words. My head jerked up at each new sound.

I sat up and stuffed a cookie into my mouth. Then another, then took a gulp of lukewarm pop.

The fireworks would start soon, with noise and bright lights and excitement. And I would watch from my own jungle perch, while Heather watched the sky from her jungle perch at camp. Not the way we'd planned. . . .

I pulled out another cookie. No use thinking about the way we'd planned. Tonight it was me and the boma. I would keep busy while I waited; I would *make* the time go fast. Because Bal-Za was waiting too, tense and alert. I could write her story now. I knew just how she felt. This was her ordeal, her testing. The real initiation.

The flashlight, even hidden under the beach towel, brought more bugs. I could hear distant small cracks and booms and pops. And I could see little pinpricks of light blinking on and off over the river. The fireflies were coming out to watch the show, too. Any minute now, the fireworks would start. And the waiting would end.

Any minute now . . . Bal-Za was hiding in the thick jungle growth. It was hot and steamy. Eyes stared at her out of the heavy blackness. Her long thick golden hair was matted and full of leaves. She was dirty, sweaty, and hungry. She pulled herself up into a tree, trying to find a comfortable crotch to rest in, hoping that Histah was not winding his slimy body around the bole. She could not keep awake

141

any longer. She was worn out from fear. Her eyes were bloodshot; she couldn't focus any longer.

Meanwhile, in another part of the jungle, Tarzan still traveled swiftly through the upper vines, following his daughter's scent-spoor. . . .

It wouldn't be long now. Bal-Za would finally meet her real father. I could hardly wait to write the last tender scene.

BOOM! I almost dropped my pen into the river.

BOOM! A shower of red and yellow spattered the sky.

BOOM! A big circle of orange dripped color back down to the ground.

KA-BOOM! The whole sky exploded in green and gold. But the boma was so low and covered with vines, I could only see the highest fireworks. The higher roof dais would have a better view. I climbed up.

The view was great on the dais. I could see the roof of the card shop, the music shop, the apartments farther down the street. I blinked, then stared. There were *people* on those roofs. Some were sitting in lawn chairs, some spread out on blankets.

The tarmangani were up on the roofs! Watching fireworks! I crouched lower on the dais so they wouldn't see me. It was wrong, all wrong! They didn't belong up here! Who did they think they were, sitting around on rooftops as if they had bomas, too? Tarmanganis invading the upper jungle heights!

I turned my head, even started to open my mouth—then I remembered again. Heather wasn't here. I was on my own in this invasion.

142

BOOM! Red, orange, blue streaks dancing over the sky. And all those silly tarmangani kids jumping around on their rooftops and yelling and clapping.

BOOM! This one sounded different. More distant. And there weren't any fireworks with it. A dud, then.

The next one turned the whole sky gold. I pressed close to the dais and looked up at the lights, away from the tarmangani and their roofs. If I didn't look at them, or think about them, if I ignored them, maybe it wouldn't be so insulting. So *wrong*. When Heather got back and heard about this, she'd be furious.

Rumble-boom. Another dud. No lights.

Then fast, high, bright, one after another. The spectacular grand finale. The sky was all wriggling color snakes, alive and glowing.

One last super BOOM and it was over. The sparks dripped down. The sky got darker, emptier. I stayed on the dais, staring up into the darkness, waiting for the tarmangani to go back where they belonged.

Then I heard another rumble, deep and dangerous. This rumble wasn't from the cannon. And the spark that went with it wasn't fireworks. It was Ara —the lightning.

Twenty-Six

□□□

Icounted the seconds between the lightning and thunder and stuffed another cookie in my mouth. Not too close, yet. Maybe it wasn't headed this way at all.

But the next rumble was stronger. It shook the boma. I wrapped up in my beach towel, with my knees pulled up to my chest. I would be stoic. Denizens endured storms and heat and rain and hunger. Heather and I survived the fog last time.

But when the next zigzag streak flashed across the sky, I suddenly remembered something. Lightning strikes high things. Never be near a tree or close to power lines in a lightning storm, they always say at school.

I wished Heather was here. She had no right to be at camp when I needed her *here*, to plan, to—

Another flash, close enough to make one split second of pure daylight. And a rumble that shook the boma.

I couldn't see the black line of clouds. But I could feel them rolling toward me, ready to open up with roaring wind and rain and all the power they'd sucked up from the hot summer day.

The willow branches started swaying. I knew

that sign. First the breeze, a warning signal, then a few minutes later would come Asha, the wind. Storms hit hard and fast in Wisconsin.

I grabbed my backpack, stuffed my supplies in and zipped it shut with clumsy, shaking fingers.

Willow branches waved toward me like long whips in the wind.

Another Ara bolt, long and crackling. And another rumble that felt like a volcano erupting inside the boma. Any second now the sky would start its own fireworks show. I swung into the tree.

Calm down, Za. You've climbed this tree dozens of times. And this isn't nearly as dark as a real jungle would be. And there aren't any tarmangani inside the banquet room. Hang on. Go slow. You'll make it.

The next second Ara and Asha attacked together, with a blinding white light that flooded the boma, and a furious *whoosh* that bent and swayed and whipped the long branches around like dark spider arms. There was roaring everywhere, in my ears, my nose, my arms, my legs.

The willow was as weak as a weed blowing in a field. And I was a tiny bug, hanging on. A bug that whimpered like a hurt puppy and clung to the bole for dear life.

Boom, crackle! Water poured down, stinging, lashing.

"I've got to get down!" I sobbed, like a baby calling from a high chair. But the roaring was so loud, I couldn't hear my own voice.

The tree was trying to shake me off, thrashing

145

and slamming against the building, then wrenching back over the river. Tears and rain ran down my cheeks. Every muscle ached from hanging on so hard.

Inch down, Za. You can't just hang there forever. If you don't do it yourself, the storm will wash you down like mud.

I started sliding. Slowly, carefully, partly on purpose and partly because my bear hug on the bole was going. I could hear trash cans below, rolling and bumping into each other in the alley, and the river water slamming into its walls like it was an ocean.

The trash cans were closer now. If I fell, maybe I wouldn't break my neck. Maybe I wouldn't break anything. That thought gave me enough nerve to slide one leg down with my foot out like an antenna, feeling around for the next branch.

I reached it just before the next big blast of wind. It howled so hard, the main trunk shuddered and creaked. Asha was furious that I'd made it.

Another limb, then another. Then a big wide crotch. I knew that one. The lowest branch.

I could jump it. I could drop down. I—

Something hurtled down from the high darkness. It jabbed at me with sharp branches. I felt a pain in my arm, and then I let go.

More jabbing branches under me, over me, pricking my arms, legs, stomach, face. Wet trash, wet leaves mashed under my arms and cheeks.

I spat out the leaves and tried to get up. But my legs were too shaky. I fell on my face.

Why wasn't Mom here? Or Geri? Or Heather?

I needed them. I couldn't stop the shaking or the hiccups that were half-sobs, half gasps.

Another BOOM. Another Ara flash. And I was up, bumping into trash and branches, stumbling around the rolling cans through the driveway that led to Main Street. Some of the stores had canopies. Some had doorways set back from the street. Main Street had lampposts.

The first store had an alcove. I ran toward it—and right toward a man crouching against the wall.

He straightened when he saw me, smiling a leering smile that showed brown teeth. His shirt was torn and dirty; his face was stubbly.

I ran. I didn't let my legs shake, didn't let my head turn back to see if he was watching or following, didn't even stop to push the wet hair out of my eyes, didn't let the next roll of thunder push me back into another alcove. No more alcoves.

No alcoves. And no shops to hide in, either. Not this late. Joe's Bar was probably the only place still open. Joe's Bar—where that awful man probably came from. And where— My eyes looked down the other side of the street, toward the old, run-down apartments. One of them was number 111, apartment 11.

But he might be— But what other choice was there? My breath was wheezing and rattling. I was going to be sick. Home was a mile away. And there were probably more alcove men lurking in all the dark places.

"Best wishes for your twelfth birthday. Here,

147

take the jackknife, Erin. We'll get you a dress, too. Snap, snap, clap."

I ran and bawled the next two blocks to number 111. The hallway was dark and stuffy. There was only one light bulb at the top of the stairway. I could barely read the numbers on the doors. 1–2–3. I didn't dare knock on the wrong one. The people who lived in this place were probably like the man in the alcove.

8–9–10–11. I banged on it with both fists.

"Dad, are you in there? It's Erin. Let me in! Dad, open the door!" I sounded like an idiot, an hysterical idiot.

The chain rattled. The lock clicked. I kept yelling and banging.

"Open it. Open it. It's me!"

And then the heavy wooden door swung open, and he stood there in his robe, his eyes wide, surprised.

"What the—"

I fell right in the door, right into him, crying.

Twenty-Seven

◻◻◻

"**D**ocs your mother know you're here? What happened? How did you get here?" He tried three or four times. But I just kept bawling.

He put some Kleenex on my cuts. He got me a towel for my wet face and hair. And when my big sobs slowed to gulpy ones, he sent me into the bathroom with a big T-shirt, to change clothes.

His bathroom was tiny. Paint was peeling off the walls. The tub was the old-fashioned kind with legs. There was just one light bulb hanging from the ceiling, with a pull chain. The room was old and awful, but it gave me time to take a deep breath and think.

By the time I walked back out with his T-shirt flapping around me like a nightgown, I had a story all figured out.

Dad was tapping ashes into a chipped glass ashtray. My breath was still shuddery, but I could talk now.

"I was watching the fireworks. Geri and Katie were . . . somewhere else. I got caught . . . in the storm. So I ran in here. Mom thinks I'm spending the night with some friends. So she won't be worried about me."

Dad was satisfied. He hadn't had much practice lately in keeping track of us; in thinking up the right questions, like: "Who *were* you with? Don't you have better sense than to be walking by yourself in the middle of downtown at midnight on the Fourth of July?" No, Dad was out of practice with it all.

He just snuffed out his cigarette and scowled. "It's not safe, a girl your age out alone at night. Your mother ought to have better sense."

I stared. "But Dad—" I just *told* him she didn't even know about it.

". . . so tired you'll fall over if you don't get some sleep. If no one's looking for you, might as well sleep here, on the couch. We'll talk more in the morning." He shook his head, like he still couldn't quite believe the whole thing.

I tried to sleep. But his little place was stuffy and hot. There were too many creaks and hisses and rumbles. I tossed around, slipped in and out of dreams, and jerked up at every new sound. By six thirty I was ready to quit trying.

Dad was awake, too, in his bed behind a curtained partition. And he'd gotten over the shock of my showing up like a drenched kitten on his doorway. With the storm and the night over and morning light filling the room, he seemed to actually enjoy the whole thing.

"You are a sight." He shook his head, grinning.

"Go get your clothes on. There's a coffee shop up the street." He pointed his finger at me.

"Erin Go Bragh—you and I are going out for breakfast."

The street was calm now. There was no terrible wind or rain, just wet sidewalks. My still-damp clothes were like air-conditioning, turning the warm breeze into a cool one.

Dad talked the whole way. "Did you know I've got a job? Right in here, young lady." He guided me into a building, with a coffee shop on the street level.

"There's a big banquet room upstairs. This is quite a place," he said proudly.

"Hey, Al," Dad called in a big booming voice, "want you to meet my daughter, Erin." The man behind the counter smiled.

"This pretty thing your daughter, Dan?"

"I said so, didn't I?" He looked very pleased, leading me toward a booth by the back window. "I help set up banquets in the room upstairs." His loud voice seemed to be meant for Al, as well as me. He took a long, slow drag on his cigarette, then snuffed it out and leaned back. "I started in the kitchen first, but that only lasted one day. They told me to cut up the cabbage for coleslaw, and I shredded the lettuce instead. Lettuce, cabbage, what's the difference?" He grinned. "It's all green leaves. But now I help with the banquets."

I had to grin, too. My dad wasn't like *anybody* else's Dad; that was for sure.

"Order anything you want, hear? Banana split,

151

pancakes, steak, pie à la mode, anything. Today's payday." He raised his voice again.

"Brought my girl here for breakfast, Al."

I sat farther back against the corner. It was embarrassing. But he seemed so . . . proud that I was here with him.

"Just an egg, Dad." I sounded like Katie.

Dad downed his coffee in practically one gulp. I fiddled with the sugar packets. I felt so strange. Tired, unreal. The whole night had been unreal; being in this coffee shop right now with Dad was unreal.

I laid my head back and shut my eyes for just a second. I could feel a cool breeze blowing in through the window. There was a bird singing in the tree outside. I knew that bird call. The cardinal. Heather and I had heard it from the boma, lots of times.

I opened my eyes and looked out the window. The tree outside the window was a willow. Long drooping branches swept over the panes. And—this side of Main Street had its back to the river. . . .

"Dad," I said slowly, "where are we?"

"Maddens."

Maddens. How dumb could I be? I'd have recognized it right away from the back. And maybe from the front, too, if I wasn't so tired and out-of-joint.

That willow waving its branches outside the window was the *boma* tree. That meant that right above this coffee shop was *the* banquet room. Unbelievable. And Dad. He *worked* here. Set up banquets. My dad was a tarmangani waiter.

The food came. I pulled my toast into skinny strips and dunked them in the egg yolk and stared out the window some more.

The strange feeling inside of me was not just because I was inside Maddens. It was because after last night, everything was different. The boma wouldn't ever be as high, as alone, as safe, as special. Not after that storm. Not after all those tarmanganis on the other roofs wrecked the alone-in-the-jungle feeling. It couldn't be the way it used to. Not ever again.

Dad set down his mug and took out his wallet. "Now, like I told you, today's payday. I go to work at noon. But I'm picking up my check now. And this is for you."

He held out two bills. Two ten dollar bills. I stared. "Dad—"

"They're for you. I want you to go out and buy the prettiest dress in town. It's about time you started dressing like a young lady. OK?"

It was a wish come true. But at the wrong time and in the wrong place and from the wrong person. It was as unreal as the rest of the morning.

"Cat got your tongue?" His mouth still wore that cocky smile, but his eyes were probing, serious.

And then he said it. "From now on, things are going to be different." His voice was low, firm.

I tensed. I hated those words.

"Don't listen; don't believe," buzzed the little warning alarm. "Don't fall for that line. You *know* better."

He crushed out his cigarette, still nodding and

153

talking. "I've got this job, you know; setting up parties and banquets. I've got money coming in." His voice was proud.

I swallowed hard. The alarm rang out louder, sharper: "He means it *now*. But what about later? He won't mean it later. You know that. Don't forget about later."

But it wasn't later. It was now. We were sitting in Maddens. He was buying me breakfast, giving me a present. He'd rescued me, after all.

He folded the bills and closed my fist over them. "Thanks, Dad."

"No jeans this time. Right?" He set down his coffee cup. His fingers flicked across the tabletop, like accordian pleats unfolding. 1–2–3–4 in quick rhythm.

His eyes caught mine. "You could do it, too," he said, smiling. "It just takes practice."

I shook my head. "I'll never get that one. Only this." With a little smile, I raised my hands. Snap, snap, clap, but softly, because it was a restaurant. It was like sign language, just between us. And in that moment, I knew what it meant. It meant—right now is good. Take the good now, Erin. Remember now. Here in Maddens. Believe in that.

There were too many laters to worry about, stretching ahead farther than I could reach. I couldn't do anything about them. And things wouldn't "be different around here" all at once, like magic. They never were.

But *now* was important, too. It meant he wasn't all bad, like the evil tarmanganis in the E.R.B. books.

154

And he wasn't like Tarzan, strong and perfect, either. He was somewhere in the middle, trying, hurting, caring, and "still your father."

"I'll get a dress," I said softly.

We walked out to an ordinary morning on Main Street. There were no dark figures lying in doorways, no trash or debris from the storm, no trace of the nightmare.

"I need to go to the bank." Dad dropped his cigarette and stepped on it. "I'd walk back home with you, but—" and his expression hardened. "I wouldn't be welcome. You'll be all right now, won't you?" He put his arm around my shoulder. We stood there, half-connected for a long second, then I reached over from the other side and finished the hug. Quick and hard.

"Erin, you let me know if you need anything else, you hear?"

"Thanks, Dad. For everything."

I had to turn right, toward home. He had to go left, toward the bank. I walked one block, then turned around. I could see him walking toward the bank, to cash his check.

Paycheck. It was a very dangerous word. It made my stomach tighten. Joe's was just a few doors from the bank.

Suddenly I wanted to slip behind a bench or building and watch where he went after the bank. I wanted to know. I *needed* to know.

I walked another block, very slowly, turning my head every few steps, to watch. I couldn't be sure which person was him. Well then, he wouldn't recognize me from this far away, either. I'd just get a tiny bit closer, stand by a building, and—

Spy. That's what it was. Plain old spying. And he'd just bought me breakfast and given me a present.

I wouldn't really spy, just turn around one more time, to see if I could find him in the crowd.

A white shirt and dark pants were coming out of the bank. But it was so far away. Hard as I stared, I couldn't tell which way he went.

Well, that's the way it is, Erin. The wondering, the worrying, the not knowing. That's part of it all. Just cross your fingers and start walking. That's all you can do.

I passed the men's shop, then stopped in front of the thrift store. The same lady was inside, behind the counter. I stared at her for a moment through the dirty glass. Then, on impulse, I walked in.

Of course it was still there in the junk jewelry basket. Who would buy a St. Patrick's Day badge in July—except me?

The shop lady laughed when I set it down. "We only just finished with the fireworks, honey! Are you doing your shopping early or late?"

"How much?"

"Just a dime. The pin fastener's broke." She was still chuckling to herself, ringing up the sale. "Well, why not? Ireland forever, right? I buy Christmas wrap cheap after the holidays, honey."

I just nodded and walked out with my badge. My badge. I knew what it meant. Not Ireland forever. Not anything as certain as forever.

The leprechaun knew too, sitting there with that cocky smile, tipping his hat just to me: "Keep your chin up. Leprechauns bring good luck, Erin Go Bragh."

I got home fifteen minutes later. Mom was sitting very straight in her chair, waiting for me.

"Sit down, Erin. You and I need to have a talk."

Twenty-Eight

◻◻◻

Mom should have been an FBI agent instead of a secretary. She figured it all out from just one clue. It was sitting in her lap when I walked in: the letter from the clinic saying that my records were not up to date, and I needed official camp forms and parents' signatures before they could release information.

"This was the reason for all those big plans with Heather. For Jungle Day and all that, wasn't it? To make money to go to camp."

I nodded. She'd caught me completely off guard. For once I didn't have any excuse ready.

"Erin, why didn't you tell me, if you wanted to go so badly?"

"I was trying to raise the money myself. I had bank money, and we made fifteen dollars on Jungle Day. I only needed twenty-eight more. But. . . ." I couldn't finish. I couldn't say it, about the car and the nosebleeds. I just stood there.

Mom looked at me, her lips pressed together tightly. She sighed, a long deep sigh.

"Erin, you know it's been a very hard year. Some things we just can't manage. But if you'd at least told me—" Then her voice changed.

"Where did you get that cut on your arm? And those scratches?"

Now was the time for the lie about falling down from the picnic table at the park, while I was watching fireworks with my friends.

I looked back at her. Her eyes held me like a vise. Proud knowing eyes that could see straight through a person. And suddenly I was tired of lies and half-lies.

It was time to tell the truth. "Well, you see, last night I tried to camp out at a . . . secret place. To watch fireworks. And . . . the storm. . . ."

I was still too much of a wreck to get it out, though. Just saying the words started it up again; the tears poured out with the story.

Mom looked almost ill when I finished. "You mean to tell me," she said in a low, trembling voice, "that you were walking down Main Street alone in the middle of the night in that storm!"

"It was just a few blocks to Dad's apartment. He took care of me."

"Thank God he was in good enough shape to take care of somebody besides himself for a change. And I'll just bet he blamed me that you were out. Right?"

I was surprised. "How did you know that?"

"Because he couldn't live with himself, if he blamed himself for all the things that have gone wrong in this family." Her voice was hard and bitter. "Erin, you took a terrible chance, being out on your own like that. All sorts of horrible things could have happened."

"They did." I'd been through everything in the last twelve hours. Then I remembered that face in the alcove. And I knew what she meant. "I won't do it again, ever."

"You certainly won't. Now"—her eyes bored right through me—"tell me, just where is this secret place that's only a few blocks from Dad's?"

My whole body stiffened. "Mom, I can't tell you that. Really. It's not just my secret. It's Heather's, too. And we made a pact. I just can't tell."

"I'm sorry, too. Because I can't allow you to go there again. All I know is that it's downtown—or close to it. And that's enough to know that it's not safe. Do you understand, Erin? You're to stay away from there from now on."

"Yes." It didn't hurt like it would have last week, or even last night. What I'd guessed in the coffee shop, I knew for sure, now. I'd never feel the same about the boma again.

"You've certainly been punished enough." She shook her head. Her next words were very low, more to herself than me.

"You must have really wanted to camp." Her hand brushed back my tangled hair, then rested on my shoulder, kneading at the tension and tightness.

"Try to go to sleep. Later we'll have another talk. All of us."

It wasn't until I was stretched out on my bed, almost asleep, that I remembered. I'd left my backpack, with my beach towel and Bal-Za, at Dad's.

We had a family council that night. It showed

that four heads are better than one for thinking up ideas and plans. Especially when one is as smart as an FBI agent and also has a few days of vacation coming up. And one is itching to practice her driving on country roads. And one still has fifty-seven dollars. (And twenty dollars tucked away in a drawer; but that had to go for a dress.)

When Heather got back from camp, she got in on the plan, too. Because the money in the can was half hers. We didn't talk much about Camp Firefly. She knew I'd been miserable at home, and I knew she'd been at least half-miserable up north without me. So we ignored the week as if it never happened. The Ara Project was past tense. Now there was a New Plan.

The New Plan brought out everyone's talents during the next two weeks. Heather and I discovered how to haggle prices with her mom over an old nine-by-twelve tent left over from the rummage sale. We got the price down to thirty-five dollars. I felt like a real wheeler-dealer when I talked her into throwing in the Styrofoam ice chest for free.

Mom's talent was packing the car so full with sleeping bags and food boxes and equipment and suitcases that it was like a jigsaw puzzle, with not even one square inch of space leftover.

Katie's talent was figuring out how to sit on top of two suitcases in the back seat and keep her head from going through the roof.

Matilda the Second's big feat was being able to *move* under all that weight, plus five bodies crammed in the front and back, plus Heather's suitcase tied

161

onto the top. The old car groaned and shuddered. But she held steady, all the way across town, and out onto County Trunk A, east.

Geri did pretty well on the country road. She wasn't so good at navigating, though. We zoomed right past the County P turnoff and went four miles out of our way, before she managed to turn a one-hundred-eighty degree turn right in the middle of the road.

The next turnoff, the important one, was well marked. Geri found it all by herself. With a little ladylike burp, Matilda turned onto the dirt road that led into the wilderness of the Wisconsin Kettle Moraine State Campground.

Twenty-Nine

◻◻◻

I t was embarrassing. After all, full-fledged denizens ought to be able to start a fire.

"Get another match," Heather said, throwing more twigs into the firepit. "It's *got* to start soon."

I struck the match, threw it in, and watched the tiny spark of flame slowly disappear into the blackness of the pit.

"Try adding paper." Mom handed us the leftover paper cups and plates. For two and a half minutes we had a gorgeous crackling fire.

"Hurry, stick the hot dogs on the skewers!"

"The fire's dying out!"

"We need more paper!"

Katie ran into the tent and brought out the paper towels.

"Here's a lot of paper," she cried, tearing pieces off madly and throwing them in.

"Katie—" Mom began, then shook her head with a little grin. "Oh well, we brought a lot of napkins, too."

"Hey, Geri," I yelled, "you better get over here and cook your hot dog. Our fire's only going to last as long as the paper towels!"

But Geri scooted her chair farther back, almost into the tent. "Oooh," she moaned. "Mom, rub my back again with Noxzema. I'm in *agony.*"

"It's no wonder, either, smearing cocoa butter all over yourself and frying out on the beach for three hours. I thought you had better sense, Geri!"

She groaned. "It wasn't cocoa butter. I forgot to bring it. It was margarine."

"And did you roll in cornmeal, too?" Mom said, with a look of disgust.

"What are we going to put on our toast now?" I yelled.

"Leave me alone," Geri muttered. And she did look miserable. Lobster-miserable, from head to toe.

"Poor Geri," Heather said.

I nodded. Poor dumb Geri. Out frying on the beach, when she could have been hiking in the woods, like us.

The woods. Just seeing that beautiful wild forest stretching behind our campsite had practically given me a rash. Huge trees, ferns sprouting all over the forest floor, chipmunks, a zillion birds and a lake.

"Erin, roast me another hot dog." Katie tore off the last piece of toweling and threw in the cardboard tube.

I stared at her. "You want *another* hot dog?"

She grinned. "I like 'em burnt."

I thought of all the hard-boiled eggs we'd brought in the ice chest. Katie had another new talent. She could eat hot dogs. Amazing.

I skewered the last hot dog and watched it bead

with grease, spitting and sizzling. My hands pulled away the skewer, but my eyes stayed on the fire.

The flames were dying down now, leaving a heap of red-orange crinkles, edged in black. Like velvet. I stared and stared until the rest of the world receded; there was only that glowing, writhing world inside the fire ring. Alive, warm, magical.

I don't hate fires after all. Not campfires in a shadowy woods, with the sky growing dark overhead. . . .

Geri's voice made me jump. "Drat those mosquitos. I just swatted my sunburn! I'm going in the tent!"

"We should all call it a night." Mom carried the food box over to the car.

I poked my stick into the last of the fire, turning the crinkles into hundreds of flying sparkles.

"Erin, come here." Mom held out a piece of paper. "This came in the mail right before we left. I just remembered it."

The return address was 111 Main Street, Apartment 11. The letter was on crisp stationery in neat backhand script. And formal.

Dearest Erin, I can't tell you how much I enjoyed our breakfast together. Next time it will be an evening meal in one of the banquet rooms, with all five of us. And steak and champagne. The works. As you probably know by now, you left a bag here, with a notebook. I glanced through it, to see what it was, and I found myself caught up in a very exciting jungle story. I hope that you do not mind that I took the liberty of reading it through. So this letter is also a request. When you write the conclusion, I would like to know what happens to the beautiful heroine, Bal-Za.

I gulped. Dad had *read* Bal-Za.

"What does he say?" Mom asked, watching me. "Does he still have that job at Maddens?"

"I think so. He wants to treat us all to steak and champagne." I giggled. "In the banquet room." One thing about my dad, he has class.

Mom shook her head. She looked amused, disgusted, and sad all at the same time. "A dreamer. A big dreamer," she said, then looked at me. "Like you, Erin. Except"—and she smiled a little—"I think this summer you've learned a little bit about the other side of the coin. About responsibility."

I looked down, embarrassed and pleased at the same time.

"But he's doing better, Mom. He's got a job."

"Don't get your hopes up. How many times before has he gotten better and gotten jobs? Don't kid yourself. He'll straighten up for good when he makes up his mind to, and not before." She shrugged. "But maybe you've done him some good. It's been a long time since someone really needed him. So keep in touch. Who knows how it will all come out? I've given up trying to outguess him."

Then she took a deep breath and looked straight at me.

"We just have to take it as it comes, one step at a time. Just like the move to the apartment, when we get back."

She was talking to me like she talked to Geri. Real woman-to-woman talk. So I didn't tighten my face into that moody sullen look, like I usually did when anyone mentioned moving. The move was going to happen, whether I liked it or not. The old house was sold, and the deposit was already made on an apartment six blocks away. Dad's bills would get paid.

Mom slapped at a mosquito. "We'll be eaten alive, if we stay out here any longer. Into the tent."

I unzipped the door. Mom gave the center pole a jiggle. "I wonder where that extra pole was supposed to go?"

The sleeping bags were squeezed so close together, they were practically on top of each other, with the old tent like a canvas boma around them. The flashlight gave a cozy feeling inside.

"You know, I don't think this was quite what Dr. Thomas had in mind, when he told me to slow down and take it easy," Mom said, worming her way down into her sleeping bag. "Ooh, my elbow just hit a rock." She rearranged herself a few more times. "I'll just have to keep reminding myself how much fun I'm having—" Then she smiled at me across the tent.

"How about you, tomboy? Is this kind of camping okay, after all?" Her voice was teasing, but her eyes locked with mine in the dim light. "Is it?" they asked silently, not teasing at all. "Will this make up for missing . . . the other?"

I grinned back. "It's perfect."

"Just *perfect*," Geri mimicked. She rolled over with a loud groan. "Erin, don't you dare bump into me. I'm *suffering*."

I wrinkled up my nose. "Thanks a lot for stinking up the whole tent with Noxzema."

"Just don't touch me, you hear?"

"Some denizen," Heather snickered near my ear.

I slid my way down into my sleeping bag, so that even my head was covered. Safe inside, I snapped on the flashlight and pulled Dad's letter out again.

> . . . so this letter is also a request. When you write the conclusion, I would like to know what happens to the beautiful heroine, Bal-Za.

So now Dad knew about Bal-Za. The thought gave me a very funny feeling. He even wanted to know the ending.

Well, so did I. I had tried so many times to write that big reunion scene between Bal-Za and Tarzan and finish the story. But it hadn't come, not even that night in the boma.

I knew I should finish it. But we'd all been so busy getting ready for camp, I hadn't had time. And, too, Bal-Za was feeling fuzzy, remote lately. And I couldn't just slap down any old ending. I had to feel the scene. And I couldn't. Not yet.

Maybe that was the problem. Maybe—it wasn't ready to be finished. Maybe it would take more time to know the ending. Maybe Bal-Za would just have to wait a little longer for the strong father she remembered. Maybe—we'd both have to.

I wrapped my jacket around some T-shirts to make a pillow and stretched my legs down to the bottom of my sleeping bag, carefully. But not carefully enough.

"Erin! Would you keep still!" Geri groaned. "That was my back you just bumped. What *are* you doing?"

I clasped my hands behind my head, stared up at the dark tent ceiling and said very calmly—

"For your information, I am releasing my inhibitions."